ON THE
CHURCH STEPS

SARAH C. HALLOWELL

1st WORLD
LIBRARY
Literary Society

On the Church Steps

Sarah C. Hallowell

© 1st World Library – Literary Society, 2005
PO Box 2211
Fairfield, IA 52556
www.1stworldlibrary.org
First Edition

LCCN: 2006902778

Softcover ISBN: 1-4218-1908-2
Hardcover ISBN: 1-4218-1808-6
eBook ISBN: 1-4218-2008-0

Purchase *"On the Church Steps"*
as a traditional bound book at:
www.1stWorldLibrary.org/purchase.asp?ISBN=1-4218-1908-2

1st World Library Literary Society is a nonprofit organization dedicated to promoting literacy by:

- Creating a free internet library accessible from any computer worldwide.
- Hosting writing competitions and offering book publishing scholarships.

On the Church Steps
contributed by Tim, Ed & Rodney
in support of
1st World Library Literary Society

CHAPTER I

What a picture she was as she sat there, my own Bessie! and what a strange place it was to rest on, those church steps! Behind us lay the Woolsey woods, with their wooing fragrance of pine and soft rushes of scented air; and the lakes were in the distance, lying very calm in the cloud-shadows and seeming to wait for us to come. But to-day Bessie would nothing of lakes or ledges: she would sit on the church steps.

In front of us, straight to the gate, ran a stiff little walk of white pebbles, hard and harsh as some bygone creed.

"Think of little bare feet coming up here, Bessie!" I said with a shiver. "It is too hard. And every carriage that comes up the hill sees us."

"And why shouldn't they see us?" said my lady, turning full upon me. "I am not ashamed to be here."

"Churches should always have soft walks of turf; and lovers," I would fain have added, "should have naught but whispering leaves about them."

But Bessie cut me short in her imperious way: "But we are not lovers this morning: at least," with a half-relenting look at my rueful face, "we are very good friends, and I choose to sit here to show people that we are."

"What do you care for *people* - the Bartons or the Meyricks?" as I noticed a familiar family carriage toiling up the hill, followed by a lighter phaeton. I recognized already in the latter vehicle the crimson feather of Fanny Meyrick, and "the whip that was a parasol."

"Shall I step out into the road this minute, and stop those ladies like a peaceable highwayman, and tell them you have promised to marry me, and that their anxiety as to our intimacy may be at rest? Give me but leave and I will do it. It will make Mrs. Barton comfortable. Then you and I can walk away into those beckoning woods, and I can have you all to myself."

Indeed she was worth having. With the witchery that some girls know, she had made a very picture of herself that morning, as I have said. Some soft blue muslin stuff was caught up around her in airy draperies - nothing stiff or frilled about her: all was soft and flowing, from the falling sleeve that showed the fair curve of her arm to the fold of her dress, the ruffle under which her little foot was tapping, impatiently now. A little white hat with a curling blue feather shaded her face - a face I won't trust myself to describe, save by saying that it was the brightest and truest, as I then thought, in all the world.

She said something rapidly in Italian - she is always artificial when she uses a foreign tongue - and this I caught but imperfectly, but it had a proverbial air about it of the error of too hasty assumptions.

Sarah C. Hallowell

"Well, now I'll tell you something," she said as the carriages disappeared over the top of the hill. "Fanny Meyrick is going abroad in October, and we shall not see her for ever so long."

Going abroad? Good gracious! That was the very thing I had to tell her that morning - that I too was ordered abroad. An estate to be settled - some bothering old claim that had been handed down from generation to generation, and now springing into life again by the lapsing of two lives on the other side. But how to tell her as she looked up into my face with the half-pleading, half-imperious smile that I knew so well? How to tell her *now*?

So I said nothing, but foolishly pushed the little pebbles aside with my stick, fatuously waiting for the subject to pass. Of course my silence brought an instant criticism: "Why, Charlie, what ails you?"

"Nothing. And really, Bessie, what is it to us whether Fanny Meyrick go or stay?"

"I shouldn't have thought it *was* anything. But your silence, your confusion - Charlie, you do care a little for her, after all."

Two years ago, before Bessie and I had ever met, I had fluttered around Fanny Meyrick for a season, attracted by her bright brown eyes and the gypsy flush on her cheek. But there were other moths fluttering around that adamantine candle too; and I was not long in discovering that the brown eyes were bright for each and all, and that the gypsy flush was never stirred by feeling or by thought. It was merely a fixed ensign of health and good spirits. Consequently the charm had waned, for me at least; and in my confessions to Bessie since our near intimacy it was she, not I, who had magnified it into the shadow even of a serious thought.

"Care for her? Nonsense, Bessie! Do you want me to call her a mere doll, a hard, waxen - no, for wax will melt - a Parian creature, such as you may see by the dozens in Schwartz's window any day? It doesn't gratify you, surely, to hear me say that of any woman."

And then - what possessed me? - I was so angry at myself that I took a mental *resume* of all the good that could be said of Fanny Meyrick - her generosity, her constant cheerfulness; and in somewhat headlong fashion I expressed myself: "I won't call her a dolt and an idiot, even to please you. I have seen her do generous things, and she is never out of temper."

"Thanks!" said Bessie, nodding her head till the blue feather trembled. "It is as well, as Aunt Sloman says, to keep my shortcomings before you."

"When did Aunt Sloman say that?" I interrupted, hoping for a diversion of the subject.

"This morning only. I was late at breakfast. You know, Charlie, I was *so* tired with that long horseback ride, and of course everything waited. Dear aunty never *will* begin until I come down, but sits beside the urn like the forlornest of martyrs, and reads last night's papers over and over again."

"Well? And was she sorry that she had not invited me to wait with her?"

"Yes," said Bessie. "She said all sorts of things, and,"

Sarah C. Hallowell

flushing slightly, "that it was a pity you shouldn't know beforehand what you were to expect."

"I wish devoutly that I had been there," seizing the little hand that was mournfully tapping the weather-beaten stone, and forcing the downcast eyes to look at me. "I think, both together, we could have pacified Aunt Sloman."

It *was* a diversion, and after a little while Bessie professed she had had enough of the church steps.

"How those people do stare! Is it the W - s, do you think, Charlie? I heard yesterday they were coming."

From our lofty position on the hillside we commanded the road leading out of the village - the road that was all alive with carriages on this beautiful September morning. The W - carriage had half halted to reconnoitre, and had only not hailed us because we had sedulously looked another way.

"Let's get away," I said, "for the next carriage will not only stop, but come over;" and Bessie suffered herself to be led through the little tangle of brier and fern, past the gray old gravestones with "Miss Faith" and "Miss Mehitable" carved upon them, and into the leafy shadow of the waiting woods.

Other lovers have been there before us, but the trees whisper no secrets save their own. The subject of our previous discussion was not resumed, nor was Fanny Meyrick mentioned, until on our homeward road we paused a moment on the hilltop, as we always did.

It is indeed a hill of vision, that church hill at Lenox.

Sparkling far to the south, the blue Dome lay, softened and shining in the September sun. There was ineffable peace in the faint blue sky, and, stealing up from the valley, a shimmering haze that seemed to veil the bustling village and soften all the rural sounds.

Bessie drew nearer to me, shading her eyes as she looked down into the valley: "Charlie dear, let us stay here always. We shall be happier, better here than to go back to New York."

"And the law-business?" I asked like a brutal bear, bringing the realities of life into my darling's girlish dream.

"Can't you practice law in Foxcroft, and drive over there every morning? People do."

"And because they do, and there are enough of them, I must plod along in the ways that are made for me already. We can make pilgrimages here, you know."

"I suppose so," said Bessie with a sigh.

Just then Fanny Kemble's clock in the tower above us struck the hour - one, two, three.

"Bless me! so late? And there's that phaeton coming back over the hill again. Hurry, Charlie! don't let them see us. They'll think that we've been here all the time." And Bessie plunged madly down the hill, and struck off into the side-path that leads into the Lebanon road. The last vibrations of the bell were still trembling on the air as I caught up with her again.

But again the teasing mood of the morning had come

over her. Quite out of breath with the run, as we sat down to rest on the little porch of Mrs. Sloman's cottage she said, very earnestly, "But you haven't once said it."

"Said what, my darling?"

"That you are glad that Fanny is going abroad."

"Nonsense! Why should I be glad?"

"Are you sorry, then?"

If I had but followed my impulse then, and said frankly that I was, and why I was! But Mrs. Sloman was coming through the little hall: I heard her step. Small time for explanation, no time for reproaches. And I could not leave Bessie, on that morning of all others, hurt or angry, or only half convinced.

"No, I am not sorry," I said, pulling down a branch of honeysuckle, and making a loop of it to draw around her neck. "It is nothing, either way."

"Then say after me if it is nothing - feel as I feel for one minute, won't you?"

"Yes, indeed."

"Say, after me, then, word for word, 'I am glad, *very* glad, that Fanny Meyrick is to sail in October. I would not have her stay on this side for *worlds*!'"

And like a fool, a baby, I said it, word for word, from those sweet smiling lips: "I am glad, *very* glad, that Fanny Meyrick is to sail in October. I would not have her stay on this side for *worlds*!"

CHAPTER II

The next day was Sunday, and I was on duty at an early hour, prepared to walk with Bessie to church. My darling was peculiar among women in this: her church-going dress was sober-suited; like a little gray nun, almost, she came down to me that morning. Her dress, of some soft gray stuff, fell around her in the simplest folds, a knot of brown ribbon at her throat, and in her hat a gray gull's wing.

I had praised the Italian women for the simplicity of their church-attire: their black dresses and lace veils make a picturesque contrast with the gorgeous ceremonials of the high altar. But there was something in this quiet toilet, so fresh and simple and girl-like, that struck me as the one touch of grace that the American woman can give to the best even of foreign taste. Not the dramatic abnegation indicated by the black dress, but the quiet harmony of a life atune.

Mrs. Sloman was ready even before Bessie came down. She was a great invalid, although her prim and rigid countenance forbore any expression save of severity. She had no pathos about her, not a touch. Whatever her bodily sufferings may have been - and Bessie dimly hinted that they were severe to agony at times - they were resolutely shut within her chamber door; and when she came out in the early morning, her

Sarah C. Hallowell

cold brown hair drawn smoothly over those impassive cheeks, she looked like a lady abbess - as cold, as unyielding and as hard.

There was small sympathy between the aunt and niece, but a great deal of painstaking duty on the one side, and on the other the habit of affection which young girls have for the faces they have always known.

Mrs. Sloman had been at pains to tell me, when my frequent visits to her cottage made it necessary that I should in some fashion explain to her as to what I wanted there, that her niece, Bessie Stewart, was in nowise dependent on her, not even for a home. "This cottage we rent in common. It was her father's desire that her property should not accumulate, and that she should have nothing at my hands but companionship, and" - with a set and sickly smile - "advice when it was called for. We are partners in our expenses, and the arrangement can be broken up at any moment."

Was this all? No word of love or praise for the fair young thing that had brightened all her household in these two years that Bessie had been fatherless?

I believe there was love and appreciation, but it was not Mrs. Sloman's method to be demonstrative or expansive. She approved of the engagement, and in her grim way had opened an immediate battery of household ledgers and ways and means. Some idea, too, of making me feel easy about taking Bessie away from her, I think, inclined her to this business-like manner. I tried to show her, by my own manner, that I understood her without words, and I think she was very grateful to be spared the expression of feeling. Poor soul! repression had become such a necessity to her!

So we talked on gravely of the weather, and of the celebrated Doctor McQ -, who was expected to give us an argumentative sermon that morning, until *my* argument came floating in at the door like a calm little bit of thistledown, to which our previous conversation had been as the thistle's self.

The plain little church was gay that morning. Carriage after carriage drove up with much prancing and champing, and group after group of city folk came rustling along the aisles. It was a bit of Fifth Avenue let into Lenox calm. The World and the Flesh were there, at least.

In the hush of expectancy that preceded the minister's arrival there was much waving of scented fans, while the well-bred city glances took in everything without seeming to see. I felt that Bessie and I were being mentally discussed and ticketed. And as it was our first appearance at church since - well, *since* - perhaps there was just a little consciousness of our relations that made Bessie seem to retire absolutely within herself, and be no more a part of the silken crowd than was the grave, plain man who rose up in the pulpit.

I hope the sermon was satisfactory. I am sure it was convincing to a brown-handed farmer who sat beside us, and who could with difficulty restrain his applauding comment. But I was lost in a dream of a near heaven, and could not follow the spoken word. It was just a quiet little opportunity to contemplate my darling, to tell over her sweetness and her charm, and to say over and again, like a blundering school-boy, "It's all mine! mine!"

The congregation might have been dismissed for aught

Sarah C. Hallowell

I knew, and left me sitting there with her beside me. But I was startled into the proprieties as we stood up to sing the concluding hymn. I was standing stock-still beside her, not listening to the words at all, but with a pleasant sense of everything being very comfortable, and an old-fashioned swell of harmony on the air, when suddenly the book dropped from Bessie's hand and fell heavily to the floor. I should have said she flung it down had it been on any other occasion, so rapid and vehement was the action.

I stooped to pick it up, when with a decided gesture she stopped me. I looked at her surprised. Her face was flushed, indignant, I thought, and instantly my conscience was on the rack. What had I done, for my lady was evidently angry?

Glancing down once more toward the book, I saw that she had set her foot upon it, and indeed her whole attitude was one of excitement, defiance. Why did she look so hot and scornful? I was disturbed and anxious: what was there in the book or in me to anger her?

As quickly as possible I drew her away from the bustling crowd when the service was concluded. Fortunately, there was a side-door through which we could pass out into the quiet churchyard, and we vanished through it, leaving Mrs. Sloman far behind. Over into the Lebanon road was but a step, and the little porch was waiting with its cool honey-suckle shade. But Bessie did not stop at the gate: she was in no mood for home. And yet she would not answer my outpouring questions as to whether she was ill, or what *was* the matter.

"I'll tell you in a minute. Come, hurry!" she said,

hastening along up the hill through all the dust and heat.

At last we reached that rustic bit of ruin known popularly as the "Shed." It was a hard bit of climbing, but I rejoiced that Bessie, so flushed and excited at the start, grew calmer as we went; and when, the summit reached, she sat down to rest on a broken board, her color was natural and she seemed to breathe freely again.

"Are they all hypocrites, do you think, Charlie?" she said suddenly, looking up into my face.

"They? who? Bessie, what have I done to make you angry?"

"You? Nothing, dear goose! I am angry at myself and at everybody else. Did it flash upon you, Charlie, what we were singing?"

Then she quoted the lines, which I will not repeat here, but they expressed, as the sole aspiration of the singer, a desire to pass eternity in singing hymns of joy and praise - an impatience for the time to come, a disregard of earth, a turning away from temporal things, and again the desire for an eternity of sacred song.

"Suppose I confess to you," said I, astonished at her earnestness, "that I did not at all know what I was singing?"

"That's just it! just what makes it so dreadful! *Nobody* was thinking about it - nobody! Nobody there wanted to give up earth and go straight to heaven and sing. I looked round at all the people, with their new bonnets,

Sarah C. Hallowell

and the diamonds, and the footmen in the pews up stairs, and I thought, What lies they are all saying! Nobody wants to go to heaven at all until they are a hundred years old, and too deaf and blind and tired out to do anything on earth. My heaven is here and now in my own happiness, and so is yours, Charlie; and I felt so convicted of being a story-teller that I couldn't hold the book in my hand."

"Well, then," said I, "shall we have one set of hymns for happy people, and another for poor, tired-out folks like that little dressmaker that leaned against the wall?" For Bessie herself had called my attention to the pale little body who had come to the church door at the same moment with us.

"No, not two sets. Do you suppose that she, either, wants to *sing* on for ever? And all those girls! Sorry enough they would be to have to die, and leave their dancing and flirtations and the establishments they hope to have! It wouldn't be much comfort to them to promise them they should sing. Charlie, I want a hymn that shall give thanks that I am alive, that I have you."

"Could the dressmaker sing that?"

"No;" and Bessie's eyes sought the shining blue sky with a wistful, beseeching tenderness. "Oh, it's all wrong, Charlie dear. She ought to tell us in a chant how tired and hopeless she is for this world; and we ought to sing to her something that would cheer her, help her, even in this world. Why must she wait for all her brightness till she dies? So perfectly heartless to stand up along side of her and sing that!"

"Well," I said, "you needn't wait till next Sunday to

bring her your words of cheer."

In a minute my darling was crying on my shoulder. I could understand the outburst, and was glad of it.

All athrill with new emotions, new purposes, an eternity of love, she had come to church to be reminded that earth was naught, that the trials and tempests here would come to an end some day, and after, to the patiently victorious, would come the hymns of praise. Earth was very full that morning to her and me; earth was a place for worshipful harmonies; and yet the strong contrast with the poor patient sufferer who had passed into church with us was too much for Bessie: she craved an expression that should comprehend alike her sorrow and our abundant joy.

The tempest of tears passed by, and we had bright skies again. Poor Mrs. Sloman's dinner waited long that day; and it was with a guilty sense that she was waiting too that we went down the hill at a quickened pace when the church clock, sounding up the hillside, came like a chiding voice.

And a double sense of guiltiness was creeping over me. I must return to New York to-morrow, and I had not told Bessie yet of the longer journey I must make so soon. I put it by again and again in the short flying hours of that afternoon; and it was not until dusk had fallen in the little porch, as we sat there after tea, and I had watched the light from Mrs. Sloman's chamber shine down upon the honeysuckles and then go out, that I took my resolution.

"Bessie," I said, leaning over her and taking her face in both my hands, "I have something to tell you."

Sarah C. Hallowell

CHAPTER III

"I have something to tell you;" and without an instant's pause I went on: "Mr. D - has business in England which cannot be attended to by letter. One of us must go, and they send me. I must sail in two weeks."

It was a thunderbolt out of a clear sky, and Bessie gave a little gasp of surprise: "So soon! Oh, Charlie, take me with you!" Realizing in the next instant the purport of the suggestion, she flung away from my hands and rushed into the parlor, where a dim, soft lamp was burning on the table. She sat down on a low chair beside it and hid her face on the table in her hands.

Like a flash of lightning all the possibilities of our marriage before many days - arranging it with Mrs. Sloman, and satisfying my partners, who would expect me to travel fast and work hard in the short time they had allotted for the journey, - all came surging and throbbing through my brain, while my first answer was not given in words.

When I had persuaded Bessie to look at me and to answer me in turn, I hoped we should be able to talk about it with the calm judgment it needed.

"To leave my wife - my wife!" - how I lingered on the word! - "in some poky lodgings in London, while I am spending my day among dusty boxes and files of deeds in a dark old office, isn't just my ideal of our wedding-journey; but, Bessie, if *you* wish it so -"

What was there in my tone that jarred her? I had meant to be magnanimous, to think of her comfort alone, of the hurry and business of such a journey - tried to shut myself out and think only of her in the picture. But I failed, of course, and went on stupidly, answering the quick look of question in her eyes: "If you prefer it - that is, you know, I must think of you and not of myself."

Still the keen questioning glance. What new look was this in her eyes, what dawning thought?

"No," she answered after a pause, slowly withdrawing her hand from mine, "think of yourself."

I had expected that she would overwhelm me in her girlish way with saucy protestations that she would be happy even in the dull London lodgings, and that she would defy the law-files to keep me long from her. This sudden change of manner chilled me with a nameless fear.

"If *I* prefer it! If *I* wish it! I see that I should be quite in your way, an encumbrance. Don't talk about it any more."

She was very near crying, and I wish to heaven she had cried. But she conquered herself resolutely, and held herself cold and musing before me. I might take her hand, might kiss her unresisting cheek, but she seemed frozen into sudden thoughtfulness that it was impossible to meet or to dispel.

20   Sarah C. Hallowell

"Bessie, you know you are a little goose! What could I wish for in life but to carry you off this minute to New York? Come, get your hat and let's walk over to the parsonage now. We'll get Doctor Wilder to marry us, and astonish your aunt in the morning."

"Nonsense!" said Bessie with a slight quiver of her pretty, pouting mouth. "Do be rational, Charlie!"

I believe I was rational in my own fashion for a little while, but when I ventured to say in a very unnecessary whisper, "Then you will go abroad with me?" Bessie flushed to her temples and rose from the sofa. She had a way, when she was very much in earnest, or very much stirred with some passionate thought, of pacing the parlor with her hands clasped tightly before her, and her arms tense and straining at the clasping hands. With her head bent slightly forward, and her brown hair hanging in one long tress over her shoulder, she went swiftly up and down, while I lay back on the sofa and watched her. She would speak it out presently, the thought that was hurting her. So I felt secure and waited, following every movement with a lover's eye. But I ought not to have waited. I should have drawn her to me and shared that rapid, nervous walk - should have compelled her with sweet force to render an account of that emotion. But I was so secure, so entirely one with her in thought, that I could conceive of nothing but a passing tempest at my blundering, stupid thoughtfulness for her.

Suddenly at the door she stopped, and with her hand upon it said, "Good-night, Charlie;" and was out of the room in a twinkling.

I sprang from the sofa and to the foot of the stairs, but I

saw only a glimpse of her vanishing dress; and though I called after her in low, beseeching tones, "Bessie! Bessie!" a door shut in the distant corridor for only answer.

What to do? In that decorous mansion I could not follow her; and my impulse to dash after her and knock at her door till she answered me, I was forced to put aside after a moment's consideration.

I stood there in the quiet hall, the old clock ticking away a solemn "I-told-you-so!" in the corner. I made one step toward the kitchen to send a message by one of the maids, but recoiled at the suggestion that this would publish a lovers' quarrel. So I retreated along the hall, my footsteps making no noise on the India matting, and entered the parlor again like a thief. I sat down by the table: "Bessie will certainly come back: she will get over her little petulance, and know I am here waiting."

All about the parlor were the traces of my darling. A soft little coil of rose-colored Berlin wool, with its ivory needle sheathed among the stitches, lay in a tiny basket. I lifted it up: the basket was made of scented grass, and there was a delicious sweet and pure fragrance about the knitting-work. I took possession of it and thrust it into my breast-pocket. A magazine she had been reading, with the palest slip of a paper-knife - a bit of delicate Swiss wood - in it, next came in my way. I tried to settle down and read where she had left off, but the words danced before my eyes, and a strange tune was repeating in my ears, "Good-night, Charlie - good-night and good-bye!"

One mad impulse seized me to go out under her

window and call to her, asking her to come down. But Lenox nights were very still, and the near neighbors on either side doubtless wide awake to all that was going on around the Sloman cottage.

So I sat still like an idiot, and counted the clock-strokes, and nervously calculated the possibility of her reappearance, until I heard, at last, footsteps coming along the hall in rapid tread. I darted up: "Oh, Bessie, I knew you would come back!" as through the open door walked in - Mary, Mrs. Sloman's maid!

She started at seeing me: "Excuse me, sir. The parlor was so - I thought there was no one here."

"What is it, Mary?" I asked with assumed indifference. "Do you want Miss Bessie? She went up stairs a few moments ago."

"No, sir. I thought - that is -" glancing down in awkward confusion at the key she held in her hand. She was retiring again softly when I saw in the key the reason of her discomposure.

"Did you come in to lock up, Mary?" I asked with a laugh.

"Yes, sir. But it is of no consequence. I thought you had gone, sir."

"Time I was, I suppose. Well, Mary, you shall lock me out, and then carry this note to Miss Bessie. It is so late that I will not wait for her. Perhaps she is busy with Mrs. Sloman."

Something in Mary's face made me suspect that she

knew Mrs. Sloman to be sound asleep at this moment; but she said nothing, and waited respectfully until I had scribbled a hasty note, rifling Bessie's writing-desk for the envelope in which to put my card. Dear child! there lay my photograph, the first thing I saw as I raised the dainty lid.

"Bessie," I wrote, "I have waited until Mary has come in with her keys, and I suppose I must go. My train starts at nine to-morrow morning, but you will be ready - will you not? - at six to take a morning walk with me. I will be here at that hour. You don't know how disturbed and anxious I shall be till then."

Sarah C. Hallowell

CHAPTER IV

Morning came - or rather the long night came to an end at last - and at twenty minutes before six I opened the gate at the Sloman cottage. It was so late in September that the morning was a little hazy and uncertain. And yet the air was warm and soft - a perfect reflex, I thought, of Bessie last night - an electric softness under a brooding cloud.

The little house lay wrapped in slumber. I hesitated to pull the bell: no, it would startle Mrs. Sloman. Bessie was coming: she would surely not make me wait. Was not that her muslin curtain stirring? I would wait in the porch - she would certainly come down soon.

So I waited, whistling softly to myself as I pushed the withered leaves about with my stick and drew strange patterns among them. Half an hour passed.

"I will give her a gentle reminder;" so I gathered a spray from the honeysuckle, a late bloom among the fast-falling leaves, and aimed it right at the muslin curtain. The folds parted and it fell into the room, but instead of the answering face that I looked to see, all was still again.

"It's very strange," thought I. "Bessie's pique is not apt to last so long. She must indeed be angry."

And I went over each detail of our last night's talk, from her first burst of "Take me with you!" to my boggling answers, my fears, so stupidly expressed, that it would be anything but a picturesque bridal-trip, and the necessity that there was for rapid traveling and much musty, old research.

"What a fool I was not to take her then and there! She *is* myself: why shouldn't I, then, be selfish? When I do what of all things I want to, why can't I take it for granted that she will be happy too?" And a hot flush of shame went over me to think that I had been about to propose to her, to my own darling girl, that we should be married as soon as possible *after* I returned from Europe.

Her love, clearer-sighted, had striven to forestall our separation: why should we be parted all those weary weeks? why put the sea between us?

I had accepted all these obstacles as a dreary necessity, never thinking for the moment that conventional objections might be overcome, aunts and guardians talked over, and the whole matter arranged by two people determined on their own sweet will.

What a lumbering, masculine plan was mine! *After I returned from Europe!* I grew red and bit my lips with vexation. And now my dear girl was shy and hurt. How should I win back again that sweet impulse of confidence?

Presently the household began to stir. I heard unbarring and unbolting, and craftily retreated to the gate, that I might seem to be just coming in, to the servant who should open the door.

It was opened by a housemaid - not the Mary of the night before - who stared a moment at seeing me, but on my asking if Miss Bessie was ready yet to walk, promised smilingly to go and see. She returned in a moment, saying that Miss Bessie begged that I would wait: she was hurrying to come down.

The child! She has slept too soundly. I shall tell her how insensate she must have been, how serenely unconscious when the flower came in at the window.

The clock on the mantel struck seven and the half hour before Bessie appeared. She was very pale, and her eyes looked away at my greeting. Passively she suffered herself to be placed in a chair, and then, with something of her own manner, she said hurriedly, "Don't think I got your note, Charlie, last night, or I wouldn't, indeed I wouldn't, have kept you waiting so long this morning."

"Didn't Mary bring it to you?" I asked, surprised.

"Yes: that is, she brought it up to my room, but, Charlie dear, I wasn't there: I wasn't there all night. I did shut my door, though I heard you calling, and after a little while I crept out into the entry and looked over the stairs, hoping you were there still, and that I could come back to you. But you were not there, and every-thing was so still that I was sure you had gone - gone without a word. I listened and listened, but I was too proud to go down into the parlor and see. And yet I could not go back to my room, next Aunt Sloman's. I went right up stairs to the blue room, and stayed there. Mary must have put your note on my table when she came up stairs. I found it there this morning when I went down."

"Poor darling! And what did you do all night in the blue room? I am afraid," looking at her downcast eyes, "that you did not sleep - that you were angry at me."

"At you? No, at myself," she said very low.

"Bessie, you know that my first and only thought was of the hurry and worry this journey would cost you. You know that to have you with me was something that I had scarce dared to dream."

"And therefore," with a flash of blue eyes, "for me to dare to dream it was -" and again she hid her face.

"But, my precious, don't you know that it was for *you* to suggest what I wanted all the time, but thought it would be too much to ask?" For I had discovered, of course, in my morning's work among the dead leaves on the porch, that I had desired it from the moment I had known of my journey - desired it without acknowledging it to myself or presuming to plan upon it.

At this juncture breakfast was announced, and the folding doors thrown open that led into the breakfast-parlor, disclosing Mrs. Sloman seated by the silver urn, and a neat little table spread for three, so quick had been the housemaid's intuitions.

"Good-morning, Charles: come get some breakfast. You will hardly be in time for your train," suggested Aunt Sloman in a voice that had in it all the gloom of the morning. Indeed, the clouds had gathered heavily during the parlor scene, and some large drops were rattling against the window.

I looked at my watch. After eight! Pshaw! I will let this

Sarah C. Hallowell

train go, and will telegraph to the office. I can take the night train, and thus lose only a few hours. So I stayed.

What rare power had Bessie in the very depths of her trouble, and with her face pale and eyes so heavy with her last night's vigil - what gift that helped her to be gay? Apparently not with an effort, not forced, she was as joyous and frank as her sunniest self. No exaggeration of laughter or fun, but the brightness of her every-day manner, teasing and sparkling round Aunt Sloman, coquetting very naturally with me. It was a swift change from the gloomy atmosphere we had left behind in the parlor, and I basked in it delighted, and feeling, poor fool! That the storm was cleared away, and that the time for the singing of birds was come.

I was the more deceived. I did not know all of Bessie yet. Her horror of a scene, of any suspicion that there was discord between us, and her rare self-control, that for the moment put aside all trouble, folded it out of sight and took up the serene old life again for a little space.

"Aunt Maria," said Bessie, pushing aside her chair, "won't you take care of Mr. Munro for a little while? I have a letter to write that I want him to take to New York."

Aunt Maria would be happy to entertain me, or rather to have me entertain her. If I would read to her, now, would I be so kind, while she washed up her breakfast cups?

How people can do two things at once I am sure I cannot understand; and while the maid brought in the large wooden bowl, the steam of whose household incense rose high in the air, I watched impatient for the signal to begin. When the tea-cups were all collected, and Aunt Sloman held one by the handle daintily over the "boiling flood," "Now," she said with a serene inclination of her head, "if you please."

And off I started at a foot-pace through the magazine that had been put into my hands. Whether it was anything about the "Skelligs," or "Miss Sedgwick's Letters," or "Stanley-Livingstone," I have not the remotest idea. I was fascinated by the gentle dip of each tea-cup, and watched from the corner of my eye the process of polishing each glittering spoon on a comfortable crash towel.

Then my thoughts darted off to Bessie. Was she indeed writing to her old trustee? Judge Hubbard was a friend of my father's, and would approve of me, I thought, if he did not agree at once to the hurried marriage and ocean journey.

"What an unconscionable time it takes her! Don't you think so, Mrs. Sloman?" I said at last, after I had gone through three several papers on subjects unknown.

I suppose it was scarcely a courteous speech. But Mrs. Sloman smiled a white-lipped smile of sympathy, and said, "Yes: I will go and send her to you."

"Oh, don't hurry her," I said falsely, hoping, however, that she would.

Did I say before that Bessie was tall? Though so slight that you always wanted to speak of her with some endearing diminutive, she looked taller than ever that

Sarah C. Hallowell

morning; and as she stood before me, coming up to the fireplace where I was standing, her eyes looked nearly level into mine. I did not understand their veiled expression, and before I had time to study it she dropped them and said hastily, "Young man, I am pining for a walk."

"In the rain?"

"Pshaw! This is nothing, after all, but a Scotch mist. See, I am dressed for it;" and she threw a tartan cloak over her shoulder - a blue-and-green tartan that I had never seen before.

"The very thing for shipboard," I whispered as I looked at her admiringly.

Her face was flushed enough now, but she made no answer save to stoop down and pat the silly little terrier that had come trotting into the room with her.

"Fidget shall go - yes, he shall go walking;" and Fidget made a gray ball of himself in his joy at the permission.

Up the hill again we walked, with the little Skye terrier cantering in advance or madly chasing the chickens across the road.

"Did you finish your letter satisfactorily?" I asked, for I was fretting with impatience to know its contents.

"Yes. I will give it to you when you leave to-night."

"Shall we say next Saturday, Bessie?" said I, resolving to plunge at once into the sea of our late argument.

"For what? For you to come again? Don't you always come on Saturday?"

"Yes, but this time I mean to carry you away."

A dead pause, which I improved by drawing her hand under my arm and imprisoning her little gray glove with my other hand. As she did not speak, I went on fatuously: "You don't need any preparation of gowns and shawls; you can buy your *trousseau* in London, if need be; and we'll settle on the ship, coming over, how and where we are to live in New York."

"You think, then, that I am all ready to be married?"

"I think that my darling is superior to the nonsense of other girls - that she will be herself always, and doesn't need any masquerade of wedding finery."

"You think, then," coldly and drawing her hand away, "that I am different from other girls?" and the scarlet deepened on her cheek. "You think I say and do things other girls would not?"

"My darling, what nonsense! You say and do things that other girls *cannot*, nor could if they tried a thousand years."

"Thanks for the compliment! It has at least the merit of dubiousness. Now, Charlie, if you mention Europe once in this walk I shall be seriously offended. Do let us have a little peace and a quiet talk."

"Why, what on earth can we talk about until this is settled? I can't go back to New York, and engage our passage, and go to see Judge Hubbard - I suppose you were writing to him this morning?"

She did not answer, but seemed bent on making the dainty print of her foot in the moist earth of the road, taking each step carefully, as though it were the one important and engrossing thing in life.

"- Unless," I went on, "you tell me you will be ready to go back with me this day week. You see, Bessie dear, I *must* sail on the fixed day. And if we talk it over now and settle it all, it will save no end of writing to and fro."

"Good-morning!" said a gay voice behind us - Fanny Meyrick's voice. She was just coming out of one of the small houses on the roadside. "Don't you want some company? I've been to call on my washerwoman, and I'm so glad I've met you. Such an English morning! Shall I walk with you?"

CHAPTER V

If I could have changed places with Fidget, I could scarce have expressed my disapproval of the new-comer more vehemently than he. Miss Meyrick seemed quite annoyed at the little dog's uncalled-for snapping and barking, and shook her umbrella at him in vain. I was obliged to take him in hand myself at last, and to stand in the road and order him to "Go home!" while the two young ladies walked on, apparently the best of friends.

When I rejoined them Fanny Meyrick was talking fast and unconnectedly, as was her habit: "Yes, lodgings in London - the dearest old house in Clarges street. Such a butler! He looks like a member of Parliament. We stayed there once before for three days. I am just going to settle into an English girl. Had enough of the Continent. Never do see England now-a-days, nobody. All rush off. So papa is going to have a comfortable time. Embassy? Oh, I know the general well."

I looked beseechingly at Bessie. Why wouldn't she say that we too would be there in London lodgings? Perhaps, then, Fanny Meyrick might take the hint and leave us soon.

But Bessie gave no sign, and I relapsed into a somewhat impatient *resume* of my own affairs. Yes:

Sarah C. Hallowell

married quietly on Saturday; leave here on Monday morning train; take, yes, Wednesday's steamer. I could arrange it with my law-partners to be absent a little longer perhaps, that there might be some little rest and romance about the wedding-journey.

Two or three times in the course of that morning - for she stayed with us all the morning - Fanny Meyrick rallied me on my preoccupation and silence: "He didn't use to be so, Bessie, years ago, I assure you. It's very disagreeable, sir - not an improvement by any means."

Then - I think without any malice prepense, simply the unreasoning rattle of a belle of two seasons - she plunged into a description of a certain fete at Blankkill on the Hudson, the occasion of our first acquaintance: "He was so young, Bessie, you can't imagine, and blushed so beautifully that all the girls were jealous as could be. We were very good friends - weren't we? - all that summer?"

"And are still, I hope," said I with my most sweeping bow. "What have I done to forfeit Miss Meyrick's esteem?"

"Nothing, except that you used to find your way oftener to Meyrick Place than you do now. Well, I won't scold you for that: I shall make up for that on the other side."

What did she mean? She had no other meaning than that she would have such compensation in English society that her American admirers would not be missed. She did not know of my going abroad.

But Bessie darted a quick glance from her to me, and

back again to her, as though some dawning suspicion had come to her. "I hope," she said quietly, "that you may have a pleasant winter. It will be delightful, won't it, Charlie?"

"Oh, very!" I answered, but half noting the under-meaning of her words, my mind running on deck state-rooms and the like.

"Charlie," said Miss Meyrick suddenly, "do you remember what happened two years ago to-day?"

"No, I think not."

Taking out a little book bound in Russia leather and tipped with gold, she handed it to Bessie, who ran her eye down the page: it was open at September 28th.

"Read it," said Fanny, settling herself composedly in her shawl, and leaning back against a tree with half-shut eyes.

"'*September 28th*'" Bessie read, in clear tones which had a strange constraint in them, "'Charlie Munro saved my life. I shall love him for ever and ever. We were out in a boat, we two, on the Hudson - moonlight - I was rowing. Dropt my oar into the water. Leaned out after it and upset the boat. Charlie caught me and swam with me to shore.'"

A dead silence as Bessie closed the book and held it in her hand.

"Oh," said I lightly, "that isn't worth chronicling - that! It was no question of saving lives. The New York boat was coming up, if I remember."

Sarah C. Hallowell

"Yes, it was in trying to steer away from it that I dropped my oar."

"So you see it would have picked us up, any how. There was nothing but the ducking to remember."

"Such a figure, Bessie! Imagine us running along the road to the gate! I could scarcely move for my dripping skirts; and we frightened papa so when we stepped up on the piazza out of the moonlight!"

To stop this torrent of reminiscences, which, though of nothings, I could see was bringing the red spot to Bessie's cheek, I put out my hand for the book: "Let me write something down to-day;" and I hastily scribbled: "*September* 28. Charles Munro and Bessie Stewart, to sail for Europe in ten days, ask of their friend Fanny Meyrick her warm congratulations."

"Will that do?" I whispered as I handed the book to Bessie.

"Not at all," said Bessie scornfully and coldly, tearing out the leaf as she spoke and crumpling it in her hand. - "Sorry to spoil your book, Fanny dear, but the sentiment would have spoiled it more. Let us go home."

As we passed the hotel on that dreary walk home, Fanny would have left us, but Bessie clung to her and whispered something in a pleading voice, begging her, evidently, to come home with us.

"If Mr. Munro will take word to papa," she said, indicating that worthy, who sat on the upper piazza smoking his pipe.

"We will walk on," said Bessie coldly. "Come, Fanny dear."

Strange, thought I as I turned on my heel, this sudden fond intimacy! Bessie is angry. Why did I never tell her of the ducking? And yet when I remembered how Fanny had clung to me, how after we had reached the shore I had been forced to remind her that it was no time for sentimental gratitude when we both were shivering, I could see why I had refrained from mentioning it to Bessie until our closer confidences would allow of it.

No man, unless he be a downright coxcomb, will ever admit to one woman that another woman has loved him. To his wife - perhaps. But how much Fanny Meyrick cared for me I had never sought to know. After the dismal ending of that moonlight boat-row - I had been already disenchanted for some time before - I had scarce called at Meyrick Place more than civility required. The young lady was so inclined to exaggerate the circumstance, to hail me as her deliverer, that I felt like the hero of a melodrama whenever we met. And after I had met Bessie there were pleasanter things to think about - much pleasanter.

How exasperating girls can be when they try! I had had my *conge* for the walk home, I knew, and I was vexed enough to accept it and stay at the hotel to dinner.

"I will not be played upon in this way. Bessie knows that I stayed over the morning train just to be with her, and piled up for to-morrow no end of work, as well as sarcastic remarks from D. & Co. If she chooses to show off her affection for Fanny Meyrick in these few hours that we have together - Fanny Meyrick whom she *hated* yesterday - she may enjoy her friendship undisturbed by me."

So I loitered with my cigar after dinner, and took a nap on the sofa in my room. I was piqued, and did not care to conceal it. As the clock struck five I bethought me it was time to betake me to the Sloman cottage. A sound of wheels and a carriage turning brought me to the window. The two young ladies were driving off in Fanny Meyrick's phaeton, having evidently come to the hotel and waited while it was being made ready.

"Pique for pique! Serves me right, I suppose."

Evening found me at the Sloman cottage, waiting with Mrs. Sloman by the tea-table. Why do I always remember her, sitting monumental by the silver urn?

"The girls are very late to-night."

"Yes." I was beginning to be uneasy. It was nearing train-time again.

"Such lovely moonlight, I suppose, has tempted them, or they may be staying at Foxcroft to tea."

Indeed? I looked at my watch: I had ten minutes.

A sound of wheels: the phaeton drove up.

"Oh, Charlie," said Bessie as she sprang out, "you bad boy! you'll miss your train again. Fanny here will drive you to the hotel. Jump in, quick!"

And as the moonlight shone full on her face I looked inquiringly into her eyes.

"The letter," I said, "for Judge Hubbard?" hoping that she would go to the house for it, and then I could follow her for a word.

"Oh! I had almost forgotten. Here it is;" and she drew it from her pocket and held it out to me in her gloved hand. I pressed the hand to my lips, riding-glove and all, and sprang in beside Fanny, who was with some difficulty making her horse stand still.

"Good-bye!" from the little figure at the gate. "Don't forget, Fanny, to-morrow at ten;" and we were off.

By the wretched kerosene lamp of the car, going down, I read my letter, for it was for me: "I will not go to Europe, and I forbid you to mention it again. I shall never, never forget that *I* proposed it, and that you - *accepted* it. Come up to Lenox once more before you go."

This was written in ink, and was sealed. It was the morning's note. But across the envelope these words were written in pencil: "Go to Europe with Fanny Meyrick, and come up to Lenox, both of you, when you return."

CHAPTER VI

I had a busy week of it in New York - copying out instructions, taking notes of marriages and inter-marriages in 1690, and writing each day a long, pleading letter to Bessie. There was a double strain upon me: all the arrangements for my client's claims, and in an undercurrent the arguments to overcome Bessie's decision, went on in my brain side by side.

I could not, I wrote to her, make the voyage without her. It would be the shipwreck of all my new hopes. It was cruel in her to have raised such hopes unless she was willing to fulfill them: it made the separation all the harder. I could not and would not give up the plan. "I have engaged our passage in the Wednesday's steamer: say yes, dear child, and I will write to Dr. Wilder from here."

I could not leave for Lenox before Saturday morning, and I hoped to be married on the evening of that day. But to all my pleading came "No," simply written across a sheet of note-paper in my darling's graceful hand.

Well, I would go up on the Saturday, nevertheless. She would surely yield when she saw me faithful to my word.

"I shall be a sorry-looking bridegroom," I thought as I surveyed myself in the little mirror at the office. It was Friday night, and we were shutting up. We had worked late by gaslight, all the clerks had gone home long ago, and only the porter remained, half asleep on a chair in the hall.

It was striking nine as I gathered up my bundle of papers and thrust them into a bag. I was rid of them for three days at least. "Bill, you may lock up now," I said, tapping the sleepy porter on the shoulder.

"Oh, Mr. Munro, shure here's a card for yees," handing me a lady's card.

"Who left it, Bill?" I hurriedly asked, taking it to the flaring gaslight on the stairway.

"Two ladies in a carriage - an old 'un and a pretty young lady, shure. They charged me giv' it yees, and druv' off."

"And why didn't you bring it in, you blockhead?" I shouted, for it was Bessie Stewart's card. On it was written in pencil: "Westminster Hotel. On our way through New York. Leave on the 8 train for the South to-night. Come up to dinner."

The eight-o'clock train, and it was now striking nine!

"Shure, Mr. Charles, you had said you was not to be disturbed on no account, and that I was to bring in no messages."

"Did you tell those ladies that? What time were they here?"

"About five o'clock - just after you had shut the dure, and the clerks was gone. Indeed, and they didn't wait for no reply, but hearin' you were in there, they druv' off the minute they give me the card. The pretty young lady didn't like the looks of our office, I reckon."

It was of no use to storm at Bill. He had simply obeyed orders like a faithful machine. So, after a hot five minutes, I rushed up to the Westminster. Perhaps they had not gone. Bessie would know there was a mistake, and would wait for me.

But they were gone. On the books of the hotel were registered in a clear hand, Bessie's hand, "Mrs. M. Antoinette Sloman and maid; Miss Bessie Stewart." They had arrived that afternoon, must have driven directly from the train to the office, and had dined, after waiting a little time for some one who did not come.

"And where were they going?" I asked of the sympathetic clerk, who seemed interested.

"Going South - I don't know where. The elder lady seemed delicate, and the young lady quite anxious that she should stay here to-night and go on in the morning. But no, she would go on to-night."

I took the midnight train for Philadelphia. They would surely not go farther to-night if Mrs. Sloman seemed such an invalid.

I scanned every hotel-book in vain. I walked the streets of the city, and all the long Sunday I haunted one or two churches that my memory suggested to me were among the probabilities for that day. They were either not in the city or most securely hid.

And all this time there was a letter in the New York post-office waiting for me. I found it at my room when I went back to it on Monday noon.

It ran as follows:

"WESTMINSTER HOTEL.

"Very sorry not to see you - Aunt Sloman especially sorry; but she has set her heart on going to Philadelphia to-night. We shall stay at a private house, a quiet boarding-house; for aunt goes to consult Dr. R - there, and wishes to be very retired. I shall not give you our address: as you sail so soon, it would not be worth while to come over. I will write you on the other side.

B.S."

Where's a Philadelphia directory? Where is this Dr. R - - ? I find him, sure enough - such a number Walnut street. Time is precious - Monday noon!

"I'll transfer my berth to the Saturday steamer: that will do as well. Can't help it if they do scold at the office."

To drive to the Cunard company's office and make the transfer took some little time, but was not this my wedding holiday? I sighed as I again took my seat in the car at Jersey City. On this golden Monday after-noon I should have been slowly coming down the Housatonic Valley, with my dear little wife beside me. Instead, the unfamiliar train, and the fat man at my side reading a campaign newspaper, and shaking his huge sides over some broad burlesque.

The celebrated surgeon, Dr. R -, was not at home in answer to my ring on Monday evening.

"How soon will he be in? I will wait."

"He can see no patients to-night sir," said the man; "and he may not be home until midnight."

"But I am an *im*patient," I might have urged, when a carriage dashed up to the door. A slight little man descended, and came slowly up the steps.

"Dr. R -?" I said inquiringly.

"Yes, sir."

"Just one minute, doctor, if you please. I only want to get an address from you."

He scanned me from head to foot: "Walk into my office, young man."

I might have wondered at the brusqueness of his manner had I not caught a glimpse of myself in the mirror over the mantelshelf. Dusty and worn, and with a keen look of anxiety showing out of every feature, I should scarcely have recognized myself.

I explained as collectedly as possible that I wanted the address of one of his patients, a dear old friend of mine, whom I had missed as she passed through New York, and that, as I was about to sail for Europe in a few days, I had rushed over to bid her good-bye. "Mrs. Antoinette Sloman, it is, doctor."

The doctor eyed me keenly: he put out his hand to the little silver bell that stood on the table and tapped it sharply. The servant appeared at the door: "Let the carriage wait, James."

Again the watchful, keen expression. Did he think me an escaped lunatic, or that I had an intent to rob the old lady? Apparently the scrutiny was satisfactory, for he took out a little black book from his pocket, and turning over the leaves, said, "Certainly, here it is - No. 30 Elm street, West Philadelphia."

Over the river, then, again: no wonder I had not seen them in the Sunday's search.

"I will take you over," said Dr. R -, replacing the book in his pocket again. "Mrs. Sloman is on my list. Wait till I eat a biscuit, and I'll drive you over in my carriage."

Shrewd little man! thought I: if I am a convict or a lunatic with designs on Mrs. Sloman, he is going to be there to see.

"Till he ate a biscuit?" I should think so. To his invitation, most courteously urged, that I should come and share his supper - "You've just come from the train, and you won't get back to your hotel for two hours, at least" - I yielded a ready acceptance, for I was really very hungry: I forget whether I had eaten anything all day.

But the biscuit proved to be an elegant little supper served in glittering plate, and the doctor lounged over the tempting bivalves until I could scarce conceal my impatience.

Sarah C. Hallowell

"Do you chance to know," he said carelessly, as at last we rose from the table and he flung his napkin down, "Mrs. Sloman's niece, Miss Stewart?"

"Excellently well," I said smiling: "in fact, I believe I am engaged to be married to her."

"My dear fellow," said the doctor, bursting out laughing, "I am delighted to hear it! Take my carriage and go. I saw you were a lawyer, and you looked anxious and hurried; and I made up my mind that you had come over to badger the old lady into making her will. I congratulate you with all my soul - and myself, too," he added, shaking my hand. "Only think! Had it not been for your frankness, I should have taken a five-mile ride to watch you and keep you from doing my patient an injury."

The good doctor quite hurried me into the carriage in the effusion of his discovery; and I was soon rolling away in that luxurious vehicle over the bridge, and toward Bessie at last.

I cannot record that interview in words, nor can I now set down any but the mere outline of our talk. My darling came down to meet me with a quick flush of joy that she did not try to conceal. She was natural, was herself, and only too glad, after the *contretemps* in New York, to see me again. She pitied me as though I had been a tired child when I told her pathetically of my two journeys to Philadelphia, and laughed outright at my interview with Dr. R -.

I was so sure of my ground. When I came to speak of the journey - *our* journey - I knew I should prevail. It was a deep wound, and she shrank from any talk about it. I had to be very gentle and tender before she would listen to me at all.

But there was something else at work against me - what was it? - something that I could neither see nor divine. And it was not altogether made up of Aunt Sloman, I was sure.

"I cannot leave her now, Charlie. Dr. R - wishes her to remain in Philadelphia, so that he can watch her case. That settles it, Charlie: I must stay with her."

What was there to be said? "Is there no one else, no one to take your place?"

"Nobody; and I would not leave her even if there were."

Still, I was unsatisfied. A feeling of uneasiness took possession of me. I seemed to read in Bessie's eyes that there was a thought between us hidden out of sight. There is no clairvoyant like a lover. I could see the shadow clearly enough, but whence, in her outer life, had the shadow come? *Between* us, surely, it could not be. Even her anxiety for her aunt could not explain it: it was something concealed.

When at last I had to leave her, "So to-morrow is your last day?" she said.

"No, not the last. I have changed my passage to the Saturday steamer."

The strange look came into her face again. Never before did blue eyes wear such a look of scrutiny.

"Well, what is it?" I asked laughingly as I looked straight into her eyes.

"The Saturday steamer," she said musingly - "the Algeria, isn't it? I thought you were in a hurry?"

"It was my only chance to have you," I explained, and apparently the argument was satisfactory enough.

With the saucy little upward toss with which she always dismissed a subject, "Then it isn't good-bye to-night?" she said.

"Yes, for two days. I shall run over again on Thursday."

CHAPTER VII

The two days passed, and the Thursday, and the Friday's parting, harder for Bessie, as it seemed, than she had thought for. It was hard to raise her dear little head from my shoulder when the last moment came, and to rush down stairs to the cab, whose shivering horse and implacable driver seemed no bad emblem of destiny on that raw October morning.

I was glad of the lowering sky as I stepped up the gangway to the ship's deck. "What might have been" went down the cabin stairs with me; and as I threw my wraps and knapsack into the double state-room I had chosen I felt like a widower.

It was wonderful to me then, as I sat down on the side of the berth and looked around me, how the last two weeks had filled all the future with dreams. "I must have a genius for castle-building," I laughed. "Well, the reality is cold and empty enough. I'll go up on deck."

On deck, among the piles of luggage, were various metal-covered trunks marked M -. I remember now watching them as they were stowed away.

But it was with a curious shock, an hour after we had left the dock, that a turn in my solitary walk on deck

Sarah C. Hallowell

brought me face to face with Fanny Meyrick.

"You here?" she said. "I thought you had sailed in the Russia! Bessie told me you were to go then."

"Did she know," I asked, "that *you* were going by this steamer?"

On my life, never was gallantry farther from my thoughts: my question concerned Bessie alone, but Fanny apparently took it as a compliment, and looked up gayly: "Oh yes: that was fixed months ago. I told her about it at Lenox."

"And did she tell you something else?" I asked sharply.

"Oh yes. I was very glad to hear of your good prospect. Do be congratulated, won't you?"

Rather an odd way to put it, thought I, but it is Fanny Meyrick's way. "Good prospect!" Heavens! was that the term to apply to my engagement with Bessie?

I should have insisted on a distincter utterance and a more flattering expression of the situation had it been any other woman. But a lingering suspicion that perhaps the subject was a distasteful one to Fanny Meyrick made me pause, and a few moments after, as some one else joined her, I left her and went to the smokestack for my cigar.

It was impossible, in the daily monotony of ship-life, to avoid altogether the young lady whom Fate had thrown in my way. She was a most provokingly good sailor, too. Other women stayed below or were carried in limp bundles to the deck at noon; but Fanny, perfectly poised, with the steady glow in her cheek, was always ready to amuse or be amused.

I tried, at first, keeping out of her way, with the *Trois Mousquetaires* for company. But it seemed to me, as she knew of my engagement, such avoidance was anything but complimentary to her. Loyalty to her sex would forbid me to show that I had read her secret. Why not meet her on the frank, breezy ground of friendship?

Perhaps, after all, there was no secret. Perhaps her feeling was only one of girlish gratitude, however needless, for pulling her out of the Hudson River. I did not know.

Nor was I particularly pleased with the companion to whom she introduced me on our third day out - Father Shamrock, an Irish priest, long resident in America, and bound now for Maynooth. How he had obtained an introduction to her I do not know, except in the easy, fatherly way he seemed to have with every one on board.

"Pshaw!" thought I, "what a nuisance!" for I shared the common antipathy to his country and his creed. Nor was his appearance prepossessing - one of Froude's "tonsured peasants," as I looked down at the square shoulders, the stout, short figure and the broad beard-lessness of the face of the padre. But his voice, rich and mellow, attracted me in spite of myself. His eyes were sparkling with kindly humor, and his laugh was irresistible.

A perfect man of the world, with no priestly austerity about him, he seemed a perpetual anxiety to the two young priests at his heels. They were on their dignity always, and, though bound to hold him in reverence as their superior in age and rank, his songs and his gay jests were evidently as thorns in their new cassocks.

Father Shamrock was soon the star of the ship's company. Perfectly suave, his gayety had rather the French sparkle about it than the distinguishing Italian trait, and his easy manner had a dash of manliness which I had not thought to find. Accomplished in various tongues, rattling off a gay little *chanson* or an Irish song, it was a sight to see the young priests looking in from time to time at the cabin door in despair as the clock pointed to nine, and Father Shamrock still sat the centre of a gay and laughing circle.

He had rare tact, too, in talking to women. Of all the ladies on the Algeria, I question if there were any but the staunchest Protestants. Some few held themselves aloof at first and declined an introduction. "Father Shamrock! An Irish priest! How *can* Miss Meyrick walk with him and present him as she does?" But the party of recalcitrants grew less and less, and Fanny Meyrick was very frank in her admiration. "Convert you?" she laughed over her shoulder to me. "He wouldn't take the trouble to try."

And I believe, indeed, he would not. His strong social nature was evidently superior to any ambition of his cloth. He would have made a famous diplomat but for the one quality of devotion that was lacking. I use the word in its essential, not in its religious sense - devotion to an idea, the faith in a high purpose.

We had one anxious day of it, and only one. A gale

had driven most of the passengers to the seclusion of their state-rooms, and left the dinner-table a desert. Alone in the cabin, Father Shamrock, Fanny Meyrick, a young Russian and myself: I forget a vigilant duenna, the only woman on board unreconciled to Father Shamrock. She lay prone on one of the seats, her face rigid and hands clasped in an agony of terror. She was afraid, she afterward confessed to me, to go to her state-room: nearness and voices seemed a necessity to her.

When I joined the party, Father Shamrock, as usual, was the narrator. But he had dropped out of his voice all the gay humor, and was talking very soberly. Some story he was telling, of which I gathered, as he went on, that it was of a young lady, a rich and brilliant society woman. "Shot right through the heart at Chancellorsville, and he the only brother. They two, orphans, were all that were left of the family. He was her darling, just two years younger than she.

"I went to see her, and found her in an agony. She had not kissed him when he left her: some little laughing tiff between them, and she had expected to see him again before his regiment marched. She threw herself on her knees and made confession; and then she took a holy vow: if the saints would grant her once more to behold his body, she would devote herself hereafter to God's holy Church.

"She gathered all her jewels together in a heap and cast them at my feet. 'Take them, Father, for the Church: if I find him I shall not wear them again - or if I do not find him.'

"I went with her to the front of battle, and we found

Sarah C. Hallowell

him after a time. It was a search, but we found his grave, and we brought him home with us. Poor boy! beyond recognition, except for the ring he wore; but she gave him the last kiss, and then she was ready to leave the world. She took the vows as Sister Clara, the holy vows of poverty and charity."

"But, Father," said Fanny, with a new depth in her eyes, "did she not die behind the bars? To be shut up in a convent with that grief at her heart!"

"Bars there were none," said the Father gently. "She left her vocation to me, and I decided for her to become a Sister of Mercy. I have little sympathy," with a shrug half argumentative, half deprecatory - "but little sympathy with the conventual system for spirits like hers. She would have wasted and worn away in the offices of prayer. She needed *action*. And she had the full of it in her calling. She went from bedside to bedside of the sick and dying - here a child in a fever; there a widow-woman in the last stages of consumption - night after night, and day after day, with no rest, no thought of herself."

"Oh, I have seen her," I could not help interposing, "in a city car. A shrouded figure that was conspicuous even in her serge dress. She read a book of *Hours* all the time, but I caught one glimpse of her eyes: they were very brilliant."

"Yes," sighed the Father, "it was an unnatural brightness. I was called away to Montreal, or I should never have permitted the sacrifice. She went where-ever the worst cases were of contagion and poverty, and she would have none to relieve her at her post. So, when I returned after three months' absence, I was shocked at the change: she was dying of their family disease. 'It is better, so,' she said, 'dear Father. It was only the bullet that saved Harry from it, and it would have been sure to come to me at last, after some opera or ball.' She died last winter - so patient and pure, and such a saintly sufferer!"

The Father wiped his eyes. Why should I think of Bessie? Why should the Sister's veiled figure and pale ardent face rise before me as if in warning?

Of just such overwhelming sacrifice was my darling capable were her life's purpose wrecked. Something there was in the portrait of the sweet singleness, the noble scorn of self, the devotion unthinking, uncalculating, which I knew lay hidden in her soul.

The Father warmed into other themes, all in the same key of mother Church. I listened dreamily, and to my own thoughts as well.

He pictured the priest's life of poverty, renunciation, leaving the world of men, the polish and refinement of scholars, to take the confidences and bear the burdens of grimy poverty and ignorance. Surely, I thought, we do wrong to shut such men out of our sympathies, to label them "Dangerous." Why should we turn the cold shoulder? are we so true to our ideals? But one glance at the young priests as they sat crouching in the outer cabin, telling their beads and crossing themselves with the vehemence of a frightened faith, was enough. Father Shamrock was no type. Very possibly his own life would show but coarse and poor against the chaste, heroic portraits he had drawn. He had the dramatic faculty: for the moment he was what he related - that was all.

Our vigilant duenna had gradually risen to a sitting posture, and drawn nearer and nearer, and as the narrator's voice sank into silence she said with effusion, "Well, *you* are a good man, I guess."

But Fanny Meyrick sat as if entranced. The gale had died away, and, to break the spell, I asked her if she wanted to take one peep on deck, to see if there was a star in the heavens.

There was no star, but a light rising and falling with the ship's motion, which was pronounced by a sailor to be Queenstown light, shone in the distance.

The Father was to leave us there. "We shall not make it to-night," said the sailor. "It is too rough. Early in the morning the passengers will land."

"I wish," said Fanny with a deep sigh, as if wakening from a dream, "that the Church of Rome was at the bottom of the sea!"

CHAPTER VIII

Arrived at our dock, I hurried off to catch the train for London. The Meyricks lingered for a few weeks in Wales before coming to settle down for the winter. I was glad of it, for I could make my arrangements unhampered. So I carefully eliminated Clarges street from my list of lodging-houses, and finally "ranged" myself with a neat landlady in Sackville street.

How anxiously I awaited the first letter from Bessie! As the banker's clerk handed it over the counter to me, instead of the heavy envelope I had hoped for, it was a thin slip of an affair that fluttered away from my hand. It was so very slim and light that I feared to open it there, lest it should be but a mocking envelope, nothing more.

So I hastened back to my cab, and, ordering the man to drive to the law-offices, tore it open as I jumped in. It enclosed simply a printed slip, cut from some New York paper - a list of the Algeria's passengers.

"What joke is this?" I said as I scanned it more closely.

By some spite of fortune my name was printed directly after the Meyrick party. Was it for this, this paltry thing, that Bessie has denied me a word? I turned over the envelope, turned it inside out - not a penciled

Sarah C. Hallowell

word even!

The shadow that I had seen on that good-bye visit to Philadelphia was clear to me now. I had said at Lenox, repeating the words after Bessie with fatal emphasis, "I am glad, very glad, that Fanny Meyrick is to sail in October. I would not have her stay on this side for worlds!" Then the next day, twenty-four hours after, I told her that I too was going abroad. Coward that I was, not to tell her at first! She might have been sorry, vexed, but not *suspicious*.

Yes, that was the ugly word I had to admit, and to admit that I had given it room to grow.

My first hesitancy about taking her with me, my transfer from the Russia to the later steamer, and, to crown all, that leaf from Fanny's pocket-book: "I shall love him for ever and ever"!

And yet she *had* faith in me. She had told Fanny Meyrick we were engaged. *Had she not*?

My work in London was more tedious and engrossing than I had expected. Even a New York lawyer has much to learn of the law's delay in those pompous old offices amid the fog. Had I been working for myself, I should have thrown up the case in despair, but advices from our office said "Stick to it," and I stayed.

Eating out my own heart with anxiety whenever I thought of my home affair, perhaps it was well for me that I had the monotonous, musty work that required little thought, but only a persistent plodding and a patient holding of my end of the clue.

In all these weeks I had nothing from Bessie save that first cruel envelope. Letter after letter went to her, but no response came. I wrote to Mrs. Sloman too, but no answer. Then I bethought me of Judge Hubbard, but received in reply a note from one of his sons, stating that his father was in Florida - that he had communicated with him, but regretted that he was unable to give me Miss Stewart's present address.

Why did I not seek Fanny Meyrick? She must have come to London long since, and surely the girls were in correspondence. I was too proud. She knew of our relations: Bessie had told her. I could not bring myself to reveal to her how tangled and gloomy a mystery was between us. I could explain nothing without letting her see that she was the unconscious cause.

At last, when one wretched week after another had gone by, and we were in the new year, I could bear it no longer. "Come what will, I must know if Bessie writes to her."

I went to Clarges street. My card was carried into the Meyricks' parlor, and I followed close upon it. Fanny was sitting alone, reading by a table. She looked up in surprise as I stood in the doorway. A little coldly, I thought, she came forward to meet me, but her manner changed as she took my hand.

"I was going to scold you, Charlie, for avoiding us, for staying away so long, but that is accounted for now. Why didn't you send us word that you were ill? Papa is a capital nurse."

"But I have not been ill," I said, bewildered, "only very busy and very anxious."

"I should think so," still holding my hand, and looking into my face with an expression of deep concern. "Poor fellow! You do look worn. Come right here to this chair by the fire, and let me take care of you. You need rest."

And she rang the bell. I suffered myself to be installed in the soft crimson chair by the fire. It was such a comfort to hear a friendly voice after all those lonely weeks! When the servant entered with a tray, I watched her movements over the tea-cups with a delicious sense of the womanly presence and the home-feeling stealing over me.

"I can't imagine what keeps papa," she said, chatting away with woman's tact: "he always smokes after dinner, and comes up to me for his cup of tea afterward."

Then, as she handed me a tiny porcelain cup, steaming and fragrant, "I should never have congratulated you, Charlie, on board the steamer if I had known it was going to end in this way."

This way! Then Bessie must have told her.

"End?" I said stammering: "what - what end?"

"In wearing you out. Bessie told me at Lenox, the day we took that long walk, that you had this important case, and it was a great thing for a young lawyer to have such responsibility."

Poor little porcelain cup! It fell in fragments on the floor as I jumped to my feet: "Was that *all* she told you? Didn't she tell you that we were engaged?"

For a moment Fanny did not speak. The scarlet glow on her cheek, the steady glow that was always there, died away suddenly and left her pale as ashes. Mechanically she opened and shut the silver sugar-tongs that lay on the table under her hand, and her eyes were fixed on me with a wild, beseeching expression.

"Did you not know," I said in softer tones, still standing by the table and looking down on her, "that day at Lenox that we were engaged? Was it not for *that* you congratulated me on board the steamer?"

A deep-drawn sigh as she whispered, "Indeed, no! Oh dear! what have I done?"

"You? - nothing!" I said with a sickly smile; "but there is some mistake, some mystery. I have never had one line from Bessie since I reached London, and when I left her she was my own darling little wife that was to be."

Still Fanny sat pale as ashes, looking into the fire and muttering to herself. "Heavens! To think - Oh, Charlie," with a sudden burst, "it's all my doing! How can I ever tell you?"

"You hear from Bessie, then? Is she - is she well? Where is she? What is all this?" And I seated myself again and tried to speak calmly, for I saw that some-thing very painful was to be said - something that she could hardly say; and I wanted to help her, though how I knew not.

At this moment the door opened and "papa" came in. He evidently saw that he had entered upon a scene as his quick eye took in the situation, but whether I was accepted or rejected as the future son-in-law even his penetration was at fault to discover.

"Oh, papa," said Fanny, rising with evident relief, "just come and talk to Mr. Munro while I get him a package he wants to take with him."

It took a long time to prepare that package. Mr. Meyrick, a cool, shrewd man of the world, was taking a mental inventory of me, I felt all the time. I was conscious that I talked incoherently and like a school-boy of the treaty. Every American in London was bound to have his special opinion thereupon, and Meyrick, I found, was of the English party. Then we discussed the special business which had brought me to England.

"A very unpresentable son-in-law," I read in his eye, while he was evidently astonished at his daughter's prolonged absence.

Our talk flagged and the fire grew gray in its flaky ashes before Fanny again appeared.

"I know, papa, you think me very rude to keep Mr. Munro so long waiting, but there were some special directions to go with the packet, and it took me a long time to get them right. It is for Bessie, papa - Bessie Stewart, Mr. Munro's dear little *fiancee*."

Escaping as quickly as possible from Mr. Meyrick's neatly turned felicitations - and that the satisfaction he expressed was genuine I was prepared to believe - hurried home to Sackville street.

My bedroom was always smothering in its effect on

me - close draperies to the windows, heavy curtains around the bed - and I closed the door and lighted my candle with a sinking heart.

The packet was simply a long letter, folded thickly in several wrappers and tied with a string. The letter opened abruptly:

"What I am going to do I am sure no woman on earth ever did before me, nor would I save to undo the trouble I have most innocently made. What must you have thought of me that day at Lenox, staying close all day to two engaged people, who must have wished me away a thousand times? But I did not dream you were engaged.

"Remember, I had just come over from Saratoga, and knew nothing of Lenox gossip, then or afterward. Something in your manner once or twice made me look at you and think that perhaps you were *interested* in Bessie, but hers to you was so cold, so distant, that I thought it was only a notion of my jealous self.

"Was I foolish to lay so much stress on that anniversary time? Do you know that the year before we had spent it together, too? - September 28th. True, that year it was at Bertie Cox's funeral, but we had walked together, and I was happy in being near you.

"For, you see, it was from something more than the Hudson River that you had brought me out. You had rescued me from the stupid gayety of my first winter - from the flats of fashionable life. You had given me an ideal - something to live up to and grow worthy of.

"Let that pass. For myself, it is nothing, but for the

Sarah C. Hallowell

deeper harm I have done, I fear, to Bessie and to you.

"Again, on that day at Lenox, when Bessie and I drove together in the afternoon, I tried to make her talk about you, to find out what you were to her. But she was so distant, so repellant, that I fancied there was nothing at all between you; or, rather, if you had cared for her at all, that she had been indifferent to you.

"Indeed, she quite forbade the subject by her manner; and when she told me you were going abroad, I could not help being very happy, for I thought then that I should have you all to myself.

"When I saw you on shipboard, I fancied, somehow, that you had changed your passage to be with us. It was very foolish; and I write it, thankful that you are not here to see me. So I scribbled a little note to Bessie, and sent it off by the pilot: I don't know where you were when the pilot went. This is, as nearly as I remember it, what I wrote:

> "'DEAR BESSIE: Charlie Munro is on board. He must have changed his passage to be with us. I know from something that he has just told *me* that this is so, and that he consoles himself already for your coldness. You remember what I told you when we talked about him. I shall *try* now.
>
> F.M.'

"Bessie would know what that meant. Oh, must I tell you what a weak, weak girl I was? When I found out at Lenox, as I thought, that Bessie did not care for you, I said to her that once I thought you *had* cared for me, but that papa had offended you by his manner - you weren't of an old Knickerbocker family, you know - and had given you to understand that your visits were not acceptable.

"I am sure now that it was because I wanted to think so that I put that explanation upon your ceasing to visit me, and because papa always looked so decidedly *queer* whenever your name was mentioned.

"I had always had everything in life that I wanted, and I believed that in due time you would come back to me.

"Bessie knew well enough what that pilot-letter meant, for here is her answer."

Pinned fast to the end of Fanny's letter, so that by no chance should I read it first, were these words in my darling's hand:

> "Got your pilot-letter. Aunt is much better. We shall be traveling about so much that you need not write me the progress of your romance, but believe me I shall be most interested in its conclusion.
>
> BESSIE S."

It was all explained now. My darling, so sensitive and spirited, had given her leave "to try."

CHAPTER IX

But was that all? Was she wearing away the slow months in passionate unbelief of me? I could not tell. But before I slept that night I had taken my resolve. I would sail for home by the next steamer. The case would suffer, perhaps, by the delay and the change of hands: D - must come out to attend to it himself, then, but I would suffer no longer.

No use to write to Bessie. I had exhausted every means to reach her save that of the detectives. "I'll go to the office, file my papers till the next man comes over, see Fanny Meyrick, and be off."

But what to say to Fanny? Good, generous girl! She had indeed done what few women in the world would have had the courage to do - shown her whole heart to a man who loved another. It would be an embarrassing interview; and I was not sorry when I started out that morning that it was too early yet to call.

To the office first, then, I directed my steps. But here Fate lay *perdu* and in wait for me.

"A letter, Mr. Munro, from D - & Co.," said the brisk young clerk. They had treated me with great respect of late, for, indeed, our claim was steadily growing in weight, and was sure to come right before long. I opened and read:

"The missing paper is found on this side of the Atlantic - what you have been rummaging for all winter on the other. A trusty messenger sails at once, and will report himself to you."

"At once!" Well, there's only a few days' delay, at most. Perhaps it's young Bunker. He can take the case and end it: anybody can end it now.

And my heart was light. "A few days," I said to myself as I ran up the steps in Clarges street.

"Miss Fanny at home?" to the man, or rather to the member of Parliament, who opened the door - "Miss Meyrick, I mean."

"Yes, sir - in the drawing-room, sir;" and he announced me with a flourish.

Fanny sat in the window. She might have been looking out for me, for on my entrance she parted the crimson curtains and came forward.

Again the clear glow in her cheek, the self-possessed Fanny of old.

"Charlie," she began impetuously, "I have been thinking over shipboard and Father Shamrock, and all. You didn't think then - did you? - that I cared so very much for you? I am so glad that the Father bewitched me as he did, for I can remember no foolishness on my part to you, sir - none at all. Can you?"

Stammering, confused, I seemed to have lost my

Sarah C. Hallowell

tongue and my head together. I had expected tears, pale cheeks, a burst of self-reproach, and that I should have to comfort and be very gentle and sympathetic. I had dreaded the *role*; but here was a new turn of affairs; and, I own it, my self-love was not a little wounded. The play was played out, that was evident. The curtain had fallen, and here was I, a late-arrived hero of romance, the chivalric elder brother, with all my little stock of property-phrases - friendship of a life, esteem, etc. - of no more account than a week-old playbill.

For, I must confess it, I had rehearsed some little forgiveness scene, in which I should magnanimously kiss her hand, and tell her that I should honor her above all women for her courage and her truth; and in which she would cry until her poor little heart was soothed and calmed; and that I should have the sweet consciousness of being beloved, however hopelessly, by such a brilliant, ardent soul.

But Mistress Fanny had quietly turned the tables on me, and I believe I was angry enough for the moment to wish it had not been so.

But only for a moment. It began to dawn upon me soon, the rare tact which had made easy the most embarrassing situation in the world - the *bravura* style, if I may call it so, that had carried us over such a difficult bar.

It *was* delicacy, this careless reminder of the fascinating Father, and perhaps there was a modicum of truth in that acknowledgment too.

I took my leave of Fanny Meyrick, and walked home a

wiser man.

But the trusty messenger, who arrived three days later, was not, as I had hoped, young Bunker or young Anybody. It was simply Mrs. D -, with a large traveling party. They came straight to London, and summoned me at once to the Langham Hotel.

I suppose I looked somewhat amazed at sight of the portly lady, whom I had last seen driving round Central Park. But the twin Skye terriers who tumbled in after her assured me of her identity soon enough.

"Mr. D - charged me, Mr. Munro," she began after our first ceremonious greeting, "to give this into no hands but yours. I have kept it securely with my diamonds, and those I always carry about me."

From what well-stitched diamond receptacle she had extracted the paper I did not suffer myself to conjecture, but the document was strongly perfumed with violet powder.

"You see, I was coming over," she proceeded to explain, "in any event, and when Mr. D - talked of sending Bunker - I think it was Bunker - with us, I persuaded him to let me be messenger instead. It wasn't worth while, you know, to have any more people leave the office, you being away, and - Oh, Ada, my dear, here is Mr. Munro!"

As Ada, a slim, willowy creature, with the *surprised* look in her eyes that has become the fashion of late, came gliding up to me, I thought that the reason for young Bunker's omission from the party was possibly before me.

Bother on her matrimonial, or rather anti-matrimonial, devices! Her maternal solicitude lest Ada should be charmed with the poor young clerk on the passage over had cost me weeks of longer stay. For at this stage a request for any further transfer would have been ridiculous and wrong. As easy to settle it now as to arrange for any one else; so the first of April found me still in London, but leaving it on the morrow for home.

"Bessie is in Lenox, I think," Fanny Meyrick had said to me as I bade her good-bye.

"What! You have heard from her?"

"No, but I heard incidentally from one of my Boston friends this morning that he had seen her there, standing on the church steps."

I winced, and a deeper glow came into Fanny's cheek.

"You will give her my letter? I would have written to her also, but it was indeed only this morning that I heard. You will give her that?"

"I have kept it for her," I said quietly; and the adieus were over.

CHAPTER X

Lenox again, and bluebirds darting to and fro among the maples. I had reached the hotel at midnight. Our train was late, detained on the road, and though my thoughts drove instantly to the Sloman cottage, I allowed the tardier coach-horses to set me down at the hotel. I had not telegraphed from New York. I would give her no chance to withhold herself from me, or to avoid me by running away. There was no time for her, as yet, to have read of the ship's arrival. I would take her unawares.

So, after the bountiful Nora, who presides over the comfort of her favorites, had plied me with breakfast-cakes and milk and honey, I sauntered down toward the Lebanon road. Yes, sauntered, for I felt that a great crisis in my life was at hand, and at such times a wonderful calmness, almost to lethargy, possesses me. I went slowly up the hill. The church-clock was striking nine - calm, peaceful strokes. There was no tremor in them, no warning of what was coming. The air was very still, and I stopped a moment to watch the bluebirds before I turned into the Lebanon road.

There was the little gray cottage, with its last year's vines about it, a withered spray here and there waving feebly as the soft April air caught it and tossed it to and fro. No sign of life about the cottage - doors and

Sarah C. Hallowell

windows tight shut and barred. Only the little gate swung open, but that might have been the wind. I stepped up on the porch. No sound save the echo of my steps and the knocking of my heart. I rang the bell. It pealed violently, but there were no answering sounds: nothing stirred.

I rang again, more gently, and waited, looking along the little path to the gate. There was snow, the winter's snow, lingering about the roots of the old elm, the one elm tree that overhung the cottage. Last winter's snow lying there, and of the people who had lived in the house, and made it warm and bright, not a footprint, not a trace!

Again I rang, and this time I heard footsteps coming round the corner of the house. I sat down on the rustic bench by the door. If it had been Bessie's self, I could not have stirred, I was so chilled, so awed by the blank silence. A brown sun-bonnet, surmounting a tall, gaunt figure, came in sight.

"What is it?" asked the owner of the sun-bonnet in a quick, sharp voice that seemed the prelude to "Don't want any."

"Where are Mrs. Sloman and Miss Stewart? Are they not in Lenox?"

"Miss' Sloman, she's away to Minnarsoter: ben thar' all winter for her health. She don't cal'late to be home afore June."

"And Miss Stewart? - is she with her?"

"Miss Stewart? I dunno," said the woman, with a

strange look about the corners of her mouth. "I dunno: I never see her; and the family was all away afore I came here to take charge. They left the kitchen-end open for me; and my sister-in-law - that's Hiram Splinter's wife - she made all the 'rangements. But I *did* hear," hesitating a moment, "as how Bessie Stewart was away to Shaker Village; and some does say" - a portentous pause and clearing of her throat - "that she's jined."

"*Joined* - what?" I asked, all in a mist of impatience and perplexity.

"Jined the Shakers."

"Nonsense!" I said, recovering my breath angrily. "Where is this Hiram's wife? Let me see her."

"In the back lot - there where you see the yaller house where the chimney's smoking. That's Hiram's house. He has charge of the Gold property on the hill. Won't you come in and warm yourself by the fire in the kitchen? I was away to the next neighbor's, and I was sure I hear our bell a-ringin'. Did you hev' to ring long?"

But I was away, striding over the cabbage-patch and climbing the worm-fence that shut in the estate of Hiram. Some wretched mistake: the woman does not know what she's talking about. These Splinters! they seem to have had some communication with Mrs. Sloman: they will know.

Mrs. Splinter, a neat, bright-eyed woman of about twenty-five, opened the door at my somewhat peremptory knock. I recollected her in a moment as a familiar face - some laundress or auxiliary of the Sloman family in some way; and she seemed to recognize me as well: "Why! it's Mr. Munro! Walk in, sir, and sit down," dusting off a chair with her apron as she spoke.

"Miss Stewart - where is she? *You* know."

"Miss Stewart?" said the woman, sinking down into a chair and looking greatly disturbed. "Miss Stewart's gone to live with the Shakers. My husband drove her over with his team - her and her trunk."

"Why, where was her aunt? Did Mrs. Sloman know? Why isn't Miss Bessie with her?"

"Miss' Sloman said all she could - *afterward* I guess," said the woman, wiping her eyes, "but 'twan't no use then. You see, Miss' Sloman had jined a party that was goin' to Minnesota - while she was in Philadelfy, that was - and Miss Stewart she wasn't goin'. She reckoned she'd spend the winter here in the house. Miss' Sloman's maid - that's Mary - was goin' with her to the West, and I was to hire my sister-in-law to take charge of things here, so that Miss Bessie could have her mind free-like to come and go. But afore ever Mary Jane - that's my sister-in-law - could come over from Lee, where she was livin' out, Miss Bessie comes up and opens the house. She stayed there about a week, and she had lots of company while she was here. I think she got tired. They was people that was just goin' to sail for Europe, and as soon as they went she just shut up and told me to send for Mary Jane to take care of things. So Mary Jane never see her, and perhaps she giv' you a crooked answer, sir, if you was inquirin' of her over to the cottage."

"Where's Hiram? where's your husband? Can I have his team this morning?"

"I guess so," said the sympathetic Mrs. Splinter. "He'll show you the very house he druv' her to."

Hiram was hunted for and found; and an hour later I was bowling along the Lebanon road behind the bay team he was so proud of. I had concluded to take him with me, as he could identify places and people, and I knew well what castles the Shaker houses are for the world's people outside. Hiram was full of talk going over. He seemed to have been bottling it up, and I was the first auditor for his wrath. "I know 'm," he said, cracking his whip over his horses' heads. "They be sharp at a bargain, they be. If they've contrived to get a hold on Bessie Stewart, property and all, it'll go hard on 'em to give her up."

"A *hold* on Bessie!" What dreadful words! I bade him sharply hold his tongue and mind his horses, but he went on muttering in an undertone, "Yo'll see, yo'll see! You're druv' pretty hard, young man, I expect, so I won't think nothing of your ha'sh words, and we'll get her out, for all Elder Nebson."

So Hiram, looked out along the road from under his huge fur-cap, and up hill and down. The miles shortened, until at last the fair houses and barns of the Shaker village came in sight. A sleeping village, one would have thought. Nobody in the road save one old man, who eyed us suspiciously through the back of a chair he was carrying.

"It must be dinner-time, I think," said Hiram as he drove cautiously along. Stopping at a house near the bridge: "Now this is the very house. Just you go right up and knock at that 'ere door."

I knocked. In a twinkling the door was opened by a neat Shaker sister, whose round, smiling face was flushed, as though she had just come from cooking dinner. I stepped across the threshold: "Bessie Stewart is here. Please say to her that a friend - a friend from England - wishes to see her."

"Sure," said the motherly-faced woman, for she was sweet and motherly in spite of her Shaker garb, "I'll go and see."

Smilingly she ushered me into a room at the left of the hall. "Take seat, please;" and with a cheerful alacrity she departed, closing the door gently behind her.

"Well," thought I, "this is pleasant: no bolts or bars here. I'm sure of one friend at court."

I had leisure to observe the apartment - the neatly-scrubbed floor, with one narrow cot bed against the wall, a tall bureau on which some brown old books were lying, and the little dust-pan and dust-brush on a brass nail in the corner. There was a brightly polished stove with no fire in it, and some straight-backed chairs of yellow wood stood round the room. An open door into a large, roomy closet showed various garments of men's apparel hanging upon the wall. The plain thermometer in the window casement seemed the one article of luxury or ornament in the apartment. I believe I made my observations on all these things aloud, concluding with, "Oh, Bessie! Bessie! you shall not stay here." I know that I was startled enough by the apparition of a man standing in the open closet door.

He must have been within it at my entrance, and had heard all I said.

He came forward, holding out his hand - very friendly apparently. Then, requesting me to be seated, he drew out a chair from the wall and sat down, tilting it back on two legs and leaning against the wall, with his hands folded before him. Some commonplace remark about the weather, which I answered, led to a rambling conversation, in which he expressed the greatest curiosity as to worldly matters, and asked several purely local questions about the city of New York. Perhaps his ignorance was feigned. I do not know, but I found myself relating, *a la* Stanley-Livingstone, some of the current events of the day. His face was quite intelligent, tanned with labor in the fields, and his brown eyes were kind and soft, like those of some dumb animals. I note his eyes here especially, as different in expression from those of others of his sect.

Several times during the conversation I heard footsteps in the hall, and darted from my seat, and finally, in my impatience, began to pace the floor. Kindly as he looked, I did not wish to question the man about Bessie. I would rely upon the beaming portress, whose "*Sure*" was such an earnest of her good-will. Moreover, a feeling of contempt, growing out of pity, was taking possession of me. This man, in what did he differ from the Catholic priest save in the utter selfishness of his creed? Beside the sordid accumulation of gain to which his life was devoted the priest's mission among crowded alleys and fever-stricken lanes seemed luminous and grand. A moral suicide, with no redeeming feature. The barns bursting with fatness, the comfortable houses, gain added to gain - to what end? I was beginning to give very short answers indeed to his questions, and was already meditating a foray through the rest of the house, when the door opened slowly and a lady-abbess entered. She was stiff and stately, with the most formal neckerchief folded precisely over her straitened bust, a clear-muslin cap concealing her hair, and her face, stony, blue-eyed and cold - a pale, frozen woman standing stately there.

"Bessie Stewart?" said I. "She is here - I know it. Do not detain her. I must see her. Why all this delay?"

"Dost thou mean Sister Eliza?" she asked in chilling tones.

"No, nobody's sister - least of all a sister here - but the young lady who came over here from Lenox two months ago - Bessie Stewart, Mrs. Sloman's niece." (I knew that Mrs. Sloman was quite familiar with some of the Shakeresses, and visited them at times.)

Very composedly the sister took a chair and folded her hands across her outspread handkerchief before she spoke again. I noticed at this moment that her dress was just the color of her eyes, a pale, stony blue.

"Sister Eliza: it is the same," in measured accents. "She is not here: she has gone - to Watervliet."

Can this be treachery? I thought, and is she still in the house? Will they hide from her that I am here? But there was no fathoming the woman's cold blue eyes.

"To Watervliet?" I inquired dismally. "How? when? how did she go?"

"She went in one of our wagons: Sister Leah and

Brother Ephraim went along."

"When will they return?"

"I cannot say."

All this time the man was leaning back against the wall, but uttered not a word. A glance of triumph shot from the sister's eyes as I rose. But she was mistaken if she thought I was going away. I stepped to the window, and throwing it open called to Hiram, who was still sitting in his wagon, chewing composedly a bit of straw. He leaped out in an instant, and leaning out to him I rapidly repeated in an undertone the previous conversation: "What would you do?"

"Ten chances to one it's a lie. Tell 'em you'll set there till you see her. They can't shake us off that way."

I drew in my head. The pair still sat as before. "Well," said I, "as I *must* see her, and as you seem so uncertain about it, I will wait here."

And again I took my seat. The sister's face flushed. I had meant no rudeness in my tone, but she must have detected the suspicion in it. She crimsoned to her temples, and said hastily, "It is impossible for us to entertain strangers to-day. A brother is dying in the house: we are all waiting for him to pass away from moment to moment. We can submit to no intrusion."

Well, perhaps it was an intrusion. It was certainly their house if it did hold my darling. I looked at her steadily: "Are you sure that Bessie Stewart has gone away from here?"

"To Watervliet - yea," she answered composedly. "She left here last week."

My skill at cross-examination was at fault. If that woman was lying, she would be a premium witness. "I should be sorry, madam," I said, recalling the world's etiquette, which I had half forgotten, "to intrude upon you at this or any other time, but I cannot leave here in doubt. Will you oblige me by stating the exact hour and day at which Miss Stewart is expected to return from Watervliet, and the road thither?"

She glanced across the room. Answering the look, the man spoke, for the first time since she had entered: "The party, I believe, will be home to-night."

"And she with them?"

"Yea, unless she has elected to remain."

"At what hour?"

"I cannot tell."

"By what road shall I meet her?"

"There are two roads: we generally use the river-road."

"To-night? I will go to meet her. By the river-road, you say?"

"Yea."

"And if I do not meet her?"

"If thou dost not meet her," said the lady-abbess,

answering calmly, "it will be because she is detained on the road."

I had to believe her, and yet I was very skeptical. As I walked out of the door the man was at my heels. He followed me out on to the wooden stoop and nodded to Hiram.

"Who is that, Hiram?" I whispered as he leaned across the back of a horse, adjusting some leathern buckle.

"That?" said Hiram under his breath. "That's a deep 'un: that's Elder Nebson."

Great was the dissatisfaction of the stout-hearted Splinter at my retreat, as he called it, from the enemy's ground.

"I'd ha' liked nothin' better than to beat up them quarters. I thought every minit' you'd be calling me, and was ready to go in." And he clenched his fist in a way that showed unmistakably how he would have "gone in" had he been summoned. By this time we were driving on briskly toward the river-road. "You wa'n't smart, I reckon, to leave that there house. It was your one chance, hevin' got in. Ten chances to one she's hid away som'eres in one of them upper rooms," and he pointed to a row of dormer-windows, "not knowin' nothin' of your bein' there."

"Stop!" I said with one foot on the shafts. "You don't mean to say she is shut up there?"

"Shet up? No: they be too smart for that. But there's plenty ways to shet a young gal's eyes an' ears 'thout lockin' of her up. How'd she know who was in this wagon, even if she seed it from her winders? To be sure, I made myself conspicuous enough, a-whistlin' 'Tramp, tramp,' and makin' the horses switch round a good deal. But, like enough, ef she'd be down-spereted-like, she'd never go near the winder, but just set there, a-stitchin' beads on velvet or a-plattin' them mats."

"Why should she work?" I asked, with my grasp still on the reins.

"Them all does," he answered, taking a fresh bite of the straw. "It's the best cure for sorrow, they say. Or mebbe she's a-teachin' the children. I see a powerful sight of children comin' along while you was in there talkin', a-goin' to their school, and I tried to ask some o' them about her. But the old sheep who was drivin' on 'em looked at me like vinegar, and I thought I'd better shet up, or mebbe she'd give the alarm that we was here with horses and wagon to carry her off."

I had a painful moment of indecision as Hiram paused in his narrative and leisurely proceeded to evict a fly from the near horse's ear. "I think we'll go on, Hiram," I said, jumping back to my seat again. "Take the river-road."

Hiram had brought plentiful provision for his horses in a bag under the seat. "Victualed for a march or a siege," he said as he dragged out a tin kettle from the same receptacle when we drew up by the roadside an hour after. "We're clear of them pryin' Shakers, and we'll just rest a spell."

I could not demur, though my impatience was urging me on faster than his hungry horses could go.

"I told Susan," he said, "to put me up a bit of pie and cheese - mebbe we wouldn't be back afore night. Won't you hev' some? - there's a plenty."

But I declined the luncheon, and while he munched away contentedly, and while the horses crunched their corn, I got out and walked on, telling Hiram to follow at his leisure. My heart beat fast as I espied a wagon in the distance with one - yes, two - Shaker bonnets in it. Bessie in masquerade! Perhaps so - it could not be the other: that would be too horrible. But she was coming, surely coming, and the cold prim sister had told the truth, after all.

The wagon came nearer. In it were two weather-beaten dames, neither of whom could possibly be mistaken for Bessie in disguise; and the lank, long-haired brother who was driving them looked ignorant as a child of anything save the management of his horses. I hailed them, and the wagon drew up at the side of the road.

It was the women who answered in shrill, piping voices: "Ben to Watervliet? Nay, they'd ben driving round the country, selling garden seeds."

"Did they know Bessie Stewart, who was staying in the Shaker village, in the house by the bridge?"

"Sure, there had ben a stranger woman come there some time ago: they could not tell - never heerd her name."

I was forced to let them drive on after I had exhausted every possible inquiry, trusting that Hiram, who was close behind, would have keener wit in questioning them, but Hiram, as it happened, did not come up to them at all. They must have turned off into some farm-house lane before they passed him. The afternoon wore on. It grew toward sunset, and still we kept the river-road. There was no trace of the Shaker wagon, and indeed the road was growing wild and lonely.

"I tell you what," said Hiram, stopping suddenly, "these beasts can't go on for ever, and then turn round and come back again. I'll turn here, and drive to the little tavern we passed about two mile back, and stable 'em, and then you and me can watch the road."

It was but reasonable, and I had to assent, though to turn back seemed an evil omen, and to carry me away from Bessie. The horses were stabled, and I meanwhile paced the broad open sweep in front of the tavern, across which the lights were shining. Hiram improved the opportunity to eat a hearty supper, urging me to partake. But as I declined, in my impatience, to take my eyes off the road, he brought me out a bowl of some hot fluid and something on a plate, which I got through with quickly enough, for the cool evening air had sharpened my appetite. I rested the bowl on the broad bench beside the door, while Hiram went backward and forward with the supplies.

"Now," said he as I finished at last, still keeping my eye upon the road, "you go in and take a turn lyin' down: I'll watch the road. I'm a-goin' to see this thing out."

But I was not ready to sleep yet; so, yielding to my injunction, he went in, and I seated myself, wrapped in a buffalo robe from the wagon. The night was damp and chill.

"Hedn't you better set at the window?" said the kind-hearted landlady, bustling out. Hiram had evidently told her the story.

"Oh no, thank you;" for I was impatient of walls and tongues, and wanted to be alone with my anxiety.

What madness was this in Bessie? She could not, oh she could not, have thrown her life away! What grief and disquiet must have driven her into this refuge! Poor little soul, scorched and racked by distrust and doubt! if she could not trust me, whom should she trust?

The household noises ceased one by one; the clump of willows by the river grew darker and darker; the stars came out and shone with that magnetic brilliancy that fixes our gaze upon them, leading one to speculate on their influence, and -

A hand on my shoulder: Hiram with a lantern turned full upon my face. "'Most one o'clock," he said, rubbing his eyes sleepily. "Come to take my turn. Have you seen nothing?"

"Nothing," I said, staggering to my feet, which felt like lead - "nothing."

I did not confess it, but to this hour I cannot tell whether I had been nodding for one minute or ten. I kept my own counsel as I turned over the watch to Hiram, but a suspicion shot through me that perhaps that wagon had gone by, after all, in the moment that I had been off guard.

Hiram kept the watch faithfully till five that morning,

when I too was stirring. One or two teams had passed, but no Shaker wagon rattling through the night. We breakfasted in the little room that overlooked the road. Outside, at the pump, a lounging hostler, who had been bribed to keep a sharp lookout for a Shaker wagon, whistled and waited too.

"Tell you what," said Hiram, bolting a goodly rouleau of ham and eggs, "I've got an idee. You and me might shilly-shally here on this road all day, and what surety shall we hev' that they hevn't gone by the other road. Old gal said there was two?"

"Yes, but the folks here say that the other is a wild mountain-road, and not much used."

"Well, you see they comes down by the boat a piece, or they *may* cut across the river at Greenbush. They have queer ways. Now, mebbe they *have* come over that mountain-road in the night, while you and me was a-watchin' this like ferrits. In that case she's safe and sound at Shaker Village, not knowin' anything of your coming; and Elder Nebson and that other is laughin' in their sleeves at us."

"Perhaps so."

"Now, this is my advice, but I'll do just as you say. 'Tain't no good to lay around and watch that ere house *to day*. Ef we hedn't been in such a white heat, we might just hev' hid round in the neighborhood *there* till she came along. But it's too late, for that now. Let's you and me lay low till Sunday. She'll be sure to go to meetin' on Sunday ef she's there, and you can quietly slip in and see if she is. And to shut their eyes up, so that they won't suspect nothin', we'll leave a message on one of your pasteboards that you're very sorry not to hev' seen her, drefful sorry, but that you can't wait no longer, and you are off. They'll think you're off for York: you've got York on your cards, hevn't you?"

"Yes."

"You just come and stay to my house: we'll make you comfortable, and there's only one day longer to wait. This is Friday, be'ent it? You'd best not be seen around to the hotel, lest any of their spies be about. They do a powerful sight o' drivin' round the country this time o' year. And then, you see, ef on Sunday she isn't there, you can go over to Watervliet, or we'll search them houses - whichever you choose."

There seemed no help for it but to take Hiram's advice. We drove homeward through the Shaker village, and drew up at the house again. This time the door was opened by a bent, sharp little Creole, as I took her to be: the beaming portress of the day before had been relieved at her post.

"Nay, Bessie Stewart was not at home: she would go and inquire for me when she was expected."

"No," I said carelessly, not wishing to repeat the scene of yesterday and to present myself, a humiliated failure, before the two elders again - "no: give her this card when she does come, and tell her I could stay no longer."

I had not written any message on the card, for the message, indeed, was not for Bessie, but for the others. She would interpret it that I was in the neighborhood, anxious and waiting: she would understand.

Sarah C. Hallowell

"Home, then, Hiram," as I took my seat beside him. "We'll wait till Sunday."

CHAPTER XI

"You'd better eat sum'thin'," said Hiram over the breakfast-table on Sunday morning. "Got a good long drive afore you, and mebbe a good day's work besides. No? Well, then, Susan, you put the apple-brandy into the basket, and some of them rusks, for I reckon we'll hev' work with this young man afore night."

Susan, bless her good heart! wanted to go along, and as Hiram's excitement was evidently at the highest pitch, he consented that she should occupy the back seat of the wagon: "P'raps Miss Stewart'll feel more comfortable about leavin' when she sees there's a woman along."

It was a rainy morning, and there were but few wagons on the road. Arrived at the village, we encountered one little procession after another of broad-brim straws and Shaker bonnets turning out of the several houses as we drove past. They stepped along quickly, and seemed to take no notice of us.

"Reckon we're the only visitors to-day," whispered Hiram as he stopped at the horseblock in front of the meeting-house. "You know where you hev' to set - on the left-hand side; and Susan, she goes to the right."

I followed Susan up the steps, and she hastened, as

Sarah C. Hallowell

ordered, to the right, while I took my seat on one of the back benches of the left, against the wall. It was a barn-like structure, large, neat and exquisitely chill. Two large stoves on either side possibly had fire in them - an old man who looked like an ancient porter went to them from time to time and put on coal - but the very walls reflected a chill, blue glare. The roof was lofty and vaulted, and added to the hollow coldness of the hall. The whole apartment was clean to sanctity, and in its straitness and blank dreariness no unfit emblem of the faith it embodied.

Around three sides of the hall, and facing the benches for visitors, the Shaker fraternity were ranged. The hats and straight straw bonnets hung decorously upon the wall over their heads: here and there a sky-blue shawl or one of faded lilac hung beneath the headgear. Across the wide apartment it was difficult to distinguish faces. I scanned closely the sisterhood - old, withered faces most of them, with here and there one young and blooming - but no Bessie as yet. Still, they were coming in continually through the side door: she might yet appear. I recognized my lady-abbess, who sat directly facing me, in a seat of state apparently, and close to her, on the brethren's side of the house, was Elder Nebson.

The services began. All rose, and sisters and brethren faced each other and sang a hymn, with no accompaniment and no melody - a harsh chant in wild, barbaric measure. Then, after a prayer, they entered upon the peculiar method of their service. Round and round the room they trooped in two large circles, sister following sister, brother brother, keeping time with their hanging hands to the rhythm of the hymn. Clustered in the centre was a little knot of men and women, the high dignitaries, who seemed to lead the singing with their clapping hands.

The circles passed each other and wove in and out, each preserving its unbroken continuity. I looked for Elder Nebson: could it be that he was joining in these gyrations? Yes, he was leading one of the lines. But I noticed that his hands moved mechanically, not with the spasmodic fervor of the rest, and that his eyes, instead of the dull, heavy stare of his fellows, sought with faithful yet shy constancy the women's ranks. And as the women filed past me, wringing their hands, I scrutinized each face and figure - the sweet-faced portress, the shrunken little creole ("A mulatto, she is," Hiram whispered - he had taken his seat beside me - "and very powerful, they say, among 'em"), and some fair young girls; two or three of these with blooming cheeks bursting frankly through the stiff bordering of their caps. But I saw not the face I sought.

"Them children! Ain't it awful?" muttered Hiram as a file of blue-coat boys shambled past, with hair cut square across their foreheads and bleached white with the sun. "Ain't got a grain of sense! Look at 'em! - all crowded clean out by the Shaker schools."

And surely they were a most unpromising little crowd. Waifs, snatched probably from some New York whirlpool of iniquity, and wearing the brute mark on their faces, which nothing in this school of their trans-planting tended to erase - a sodden little party, like stupid young beasts of burden, uncouth and awkward.

As the girls came round again, and I had settled it in my mind that there was certainly no Bessie in the room, I could watch them more calmly. Eagerly as I sought her face, it was a relief, surely, that it was not there. Pale to ghastliness, most of them, with high, sharpened shoulders, and features set like those of a corpse, it was indeed difficult to realize that these ascetic forms, these swaying devotees, were women - women who might else have been wives and mothers. Some of them wore in their hollow eyes an expression of ecstasy akin to madness, and there was not a face there that was not saintly pure.

It was a strange union that assembled under one roof these nun-like creatures, wasted and worn with their rigid lives, and the heavy, brutish men, who shambled round the room like plough-horses. *Wicked* eyes some of them had, mere slits through which a cunning and selfish spirit looked out. Some faces there were of power, but in them the disagreeable traits were even more strongly marked: the ignorant, narrow foreheads were better, less responsible, it seemed.

The singing ended, there was a sermon from a high priest who stood out imperious among his fellows. But this was not a sermon to the flock. It was aimed at the scanty audience of strangers with words of unblushing directness. How men and women may continue pure in the constant hearing and repetition of such revolting arguments and articles of faith is matter of serious question. The divine instincts of maternity, the sweet attractions of human love, were thrown down and stamped under foot in the mud of this man's mind; and at each peroration, exhorting his hearers to shake off Satan, a strong convulsive shiver ran through the assembly.

"Bessie is certainly not here: possibly she's still at Watervliet," I whispered to; Hiram as the concluding hymn began. "But I'll have a chance at Elder Nebson and that woman before they leave the house."

The rain had ceased for some time, and as again the wild chant went up from those harsh strained voices, a stray sunbeam, like a gleam of good promise, shot across the floor. But what was this little figure stealing in through a side-door and joining the circling throng? - a figure in lilac gown, with the stiff muslin cap and folded neckerchief. She entered at the farthest corner of the room, and I watched her approach with beating heart. Something in the easy step was familiar, and yet it could not be. She passed around with the rest in the inner circle, and, leaning forward, I held my breath lest indeed it might be she.

The circle opened, and again the long line of march around the room. The lilac figure came nearer and nearer, and now I see her face. It is Bessie!

With a cry I sprang up, but with a blow, a crash, a horrible darkness swept over me like a wave, and I knew nothing.

When I came to myself I was lying on a bed in a room that was new to me. A strong light, as of the setting sun, shone upon the whitewashed wall. There was a little table, over which hung a looking-glass, surmounted by two fans of turkey feathers. I stared feebly at the fans for a while, and then closed my eyes again.

Where was I? I had a faint remembrance of jolting in a wagon, and of pitying faces bent over me, but where was I now? Again I opened my eyes, and noted the gay patchwork covering of the bed, and the green paper curtain of the window in the golden wall - green, with a tall yellow flower-pot on it, with sprawling roses of blue and red. Turning with an effort toward the side whence all the brightness came, in a moment two warm arms were round my neck, and a face that I could not see was pressed close to mine.

"Oh, Charlie, Charlie! forgive, forgive me for being so bad!"

"Bessie," I answered dreamingly, and seemed to be drifting away again. But a strong odor of pungent salts made my head tingle again, and when I could open my eyes for the tears they rested on my darling's face - my own darling in a soft white dress, kneeling by my bedside, with both her arms round me. A vigorous patting of the pillow behind me revealed Mrs. Splinter, tearful too: "He's come to now. Don't bother him with talk, Miss Bessie. I'll fetch the tea."

And with motherly insistence she brought me a steaming bowl of beef-tea, while I still lay, holding Bessie's hand, with a feeble dawning that the vision was real.

"No," she said as Bessie put out her arm for the bowl, "you prop up his head. I've got a steddyer hand: you'd just spill it all over his go-to-meetin' suit."

I looked down at myself. I was still dressed in the clothes that I had worn - when was it? last week? - when I had started for the Shaker meeting.

"How long?" I said feebly.

"Only this morning, you darling boy, it all happened;

and here we are, snug at Mrs. Splinter's, and Mary Jane is getting the cottage ready for us as fast as ever she can."

How good that beef-tea was! Bessie knew well what would give it the *sauce piquante*. "Ready for us!"

"Here's the doctor at last," said Hiram, putting his head in at the door. "Why, hillo! are we awake?"

"The doctor! Dr. Wilder?" I said beamingly. How good of Bessie! How thoughtful!

"Not Dr. Wilder, you dear old boy!" said Bessie, laughing and blushing, "though I sha'n't scold you, Charlie, for that!" in a whisper in my ear. "It's Dr. Bolster of Lee. Hiram has been riding all over the country for him this afternoon."

"I'll go down to him," I said, preparing to rise.

"No you won't;" and Mrs. Splinter's strong arm, as well as Bessie's soft hand, patted me down again.

Dr. Bolster pronounced, as well he might, that all danger was over. The blow on my head - I must have struck it with force against the projecting window-shelf as I sprang up - was enough to have stunned me; but the doctor, I found, was inclined to theorize: "A sudden vertigo, a dizziness: the Shaker hymns and dances have that effect sometimes upon persons viewing them for the first time. Or perhaps the heat of the room." He calmly fingered my pulse for a few seconds, with his fat ticking watch in his other hand, and then retired to the bureau to write a prescription, which I was indignantly prepared to repudiate. But

Sarah C. Hallowell

Bessie, in a delightful little pantomime, made signs to me to be patient: we could throw it all out of the window afterward if need be.

"A soothing draught, and let him keep quiet for a day or so, will be all that is required. I will call to-morrow if you would prefer it."

"We will send you a note, doctor, to-morrow morning: he seems so much stronger already that perhaps it will not be necessary to make you take such a long drive."

"Yes, yes, I'm very busy. You send me word whether to come or not."

And bustlingly the good doctor departed, with Mrs. Splinter majestically descending to hold whispered conference with him at the gate.

"Charlie, I *will* send for Dr. Wilder if you are ready, for I'm never going to leave you another minute as long as we live."

"I think," said I, laughing, "that I should like to stand up first on my feet; that is, if I have any feet."

What a wonderful prop and support was Bessie! How skillfully she helped me to step once, twice, across the floor! and when I sank down, very tired, in the comfortable easy-chair by the window, she knelt on the floor beside me and bathed my forehead with fragrant cologne, that certainly did not come from Mrs. Splinter's tall bottle of lavender compound on the bureau.

"Oh, my dear boy, I have *so* much to say! Where

shall I begin?"

"At the end," I said quietly. "Send for Dr. Wilder."

"But don't you want to hear what a naughty girl - "

"No, I want to hear nothing but 'I, Elizabeth, take thee -'"

"But I've been so very jealous, so suspicious and angry. *Don't* you want to hear how bad I am?"

"No," I said, closing the discussion after an old fashion of the Sloman cottage, "not until we two walk together to the Ledge to-morrow, my little wife and I."

"Where's a card - your card, Charlie? It would be more proper-like, as Mrs. Splinter would say, for you to write it."

"I will try," I said, taking out a card-case from my breast-pocket. As I drew it forth my hand touched a package, Fanny Meyrick's packet. Shall I give it to her now? I hesitated. No, we'll be married first in the calm faith that each has in the other to-day, needing no outward assurance or written word.

I penciled feebly, with a very shaky hand, my request that the doctor would call at Hiram Splinter's, at his earliest convenience that evening, to perform the ceremony of marriage between his young friend, Bessie Stewart, and the subscriber. Hiram's eldest son, a youth of eight, was swinging on the gate under our window. To him Bessie entrusted the card, with many injunctions to give it into no other hands than the doctor's own.

Sarah C. Hallowell

In less time than we had anticipated, as we looked out of the window at the last pink glow of the sunset, the urchin reappeared, walking with great strides beside a spare little-figure, whom we recognized as the worthy doctor himself.

"Good gracious! he *is* in a hurry!" said Bessie, retiring hastily from the window; "and we have not said a word to Mrs. Splinter yet!"

We had expected the little doctor would wait below until the bridal-party should descend; but no, he came directly up stairs, and walked into the room without prelude. He took Bessie in his arms with fatherly tenderness: "Ah, you runaway! so you've come back at last?"

"Yes, doctor, and don't you let go of her until you have married her fast to me."

"Ahem!" said the doctor, clearing his throat, "that is just what I came to advise you about. Hiram told me this afternoon of the chase you two had had, and of your illness this morning. Now, as it is half over the village by this time that Bessie Stewart has been rescued from the Shaker village by a chivalrous young gentleman, and as everybody is wild with impatience to know the *denoument*, I want you to come down quietly to the church this evening and be married after evening service."

"To please everybody?" I said, in no very pleasant humor.

"I think it will be wisest, best; and I am sure this discreetest of women," still holding Bessie's hand, "will agree with me. You need not sit through the service. Hiram can bring you down after it has begun; and you may sit in the vestry till the clerk calls you. I'll preach a short sermon to-night," with a benignant chuckle.

He had his will. Some feeling that it would please Mrs. Sloman best, the only person besides ourselves whom it concerned us to please, settled it in Bessie's mind, although she anxiously inquired several times before the doctor left if I felt equal to going to church. Suppose I should faint on the way?

I was equal to it, for I took a long nap on the sofa in Mrs. Splinter's parlor through the soft spring twilight, while Bessie held what seemed to me interminable conferences with Mary Jane.

It was not a brilliant ceremony so far as the groom was concerned. As we stood at the chancel-rail I am afraid that the congregation, largely augmented, by this time, by late-comers - for the doctor had spread the news through the village far and wide - thought me but a very pale and quiet bridegroom.

But the bride's beauty made amends for all. Just the same soft white dress of the afternoon - or was it one like it? - with no ornaments, no bridal veil. I have always pitied men who have to plight their troth to a moving mass of lace and tulle, weighed down with orange-blossoms massive as lead. This was my own little wife as she would walk by my side through life, dressed as she might be the next day and always.

But the next day it was the tartan cloak that she wore, by special request, as we climbed the hill to the Ledge.

It was spring indeed - bluebirds in the air, and all the sky shone clear and warm.

"Let *me* begin," said my wife as she took her old seat under the sheltering pine. "You can't have anything to say, Charlie, in comparison with me."

There was a short preliminary pause, and then she began.

CHAPTER XII

"Well, after you wouldn't take me to Europe, you know -"

"You naughty girl!"

"No interruptions, sir. After you *couldn't* take me to Europe I felt very much hurt and wounded, and ready to catch at any straw of suspicion. I ran away from you that night and left you in the parlor, hoping that you would call me back, and yet longing to hide myself from you too. You understand?"

"Yes, let us not dwell on that."

"Well, I believe I never thought once of Fanny Meyrick's going to Europe too until she joined us on the road that day - you remember? - at the washerwoman's gate."

"Yes; and do *you* remember how Fidget and I barked at her with all our hearts?"

"I was piqued then at the air of ownership Fanny seemed to assume in you. She had just come to Lenox, I knew; she could know nothing of our intimacy, our relations; and this seemed like the renewal of some- thing old - something that had been going on before.

Sarah C. Hallowell

Had she any claim on you? I wondered. And then, too, you were so provokingly reticent about her whenever her name had been mentioned before."

"Was I? What a fool I was! But, Bessie dear, I could not say to even you, then, that I believed Fanny Meyrick was in - cared a great deal for me."

"I understand," said Bessie nodding. "We'll skip that, and take it for granted. But you see *I* couldn't take anything for granted but just what I saw that day; and the little memorandum-book and Fanny's reminis-cences nearly killed me. I don't know how I sat through it all. I tried to avoid you all the rest of the day. I wanted to think, and to find out the truth from Fanny."

"I should think you *did* avoid me pretty successfully, leaving me to dine coldly at the hotel, and then driving all the afternoon till train-time."

"It was in talking to Fanny that afternoon that I discovered how she felt toward you. She has no concealment about her, not any, and I could read her heart plainly enough. But then she hinted at her father's treatment of you; thought he had discouraged you, rebuffed you, and reasoned so that I fairly thought there might be truth in it, *remembering it was before you knew me.*"

"Listen one minute, Bessie, till I explain that. It's my belief, and always was, that that shrewd old fellow, Henry Meyrick, saw very clearly how matters were all along - saw how the impetuous Miss Fanny was -"

"*Falling in love*: don't pause for a 'more tenderer word,'

Charlie. Sam Weller couldn't find any."

"Well, falling in love, if you *will* say it - and that it was decidedly a difficult situation for me. I remember so well that night on the piazza, when Fanny clung about me like a mermaid, he bade her sharply go and change her dripping garments, and what Fanny calls 'a decidedly queer' expression came into his face. He could not say anything, poor old chap! and he always behaved with great courtesy to me. I am sure he divined that I was a most unimpassioned actor in that high-comedy plunge into the Hudson."

"Very well: I believe it, I'm sure, but, you see, how could I know then what was or was not true? Then it was that I resolved to give you leave - or rather give her leave to try. I had written my note in the morning, saying *no* finally to the Europe plan, and I scrawled across it, in lead-pencil, while Fanny stood at her horse's head, those ugly words, you remember?"

"Yes," I said: "'Go to Europe with Fanny Meyrick, and come up to Lenox, both of you, when you return.'"

"Then, after that, my one idea was to get away from Lenox. The place was hateful to me, and you were writing those pathetic letters about being married, and state-rooms, and all. It only made me more wretched, for I thought you were the more urgent now that you had been lacking before. I hurried aunt off to Philadelphia, and in New York she hurried me. She would not wait, though I did want to, and I was so disappointed at the hotel! But I thought there was a fate in it to give Fanny Meyrick her chance, poor thing! and so I wrote that good-bye note without an address."

Sarah C. Hallowell

"But I found you, for all, thanks to Dr. R -!"

"Yes, and when you came that night I was so happy. I put away all fear: I had to remind myself, actually, all the time, of what I owed to Fanny, until you told me you had changed your passage to the Algeria, and that gave me strength to be angry. Oh, my dear, I'm afraid you'll have a very bad wife. Of course the minute you had sailed I began to be horribly jealous, and then I got a letter by the pilot that made me worse."

"But," said I, "you got my letters from the other side. Didn't that assure you that you might have faith in me?"

"But I would not receive them. Aunt Sloman has them all, done up and labeled for you, doubtless. She, it seems - had you talked her over? - thought I ought to have gone with you, and fretted because she was keeping me. Then I couldn't bear it another day. It was just after you had sailed, and I had cut out the ship-list to send you; and I had worked myself up to believe you would go back to Fanny Meyrick if you had the chance. I told Aunt Sloman that it was all over between us - that you might continue to write to me, but I begged that she would keep all your letters in a box until I should ask her for them."

"But I wrote letters to her, too, asking what had become of you."

"She went to Minnesota, you know, early in February."

"And why didn't you go with her?"

"She scolded me dreadfully because I would not. But

she was so well, and she had her maid and a pleasant party of Philadelphia friends; and I - well, I didn't want to put all those hundreds of miles between me and the sea."

"And was Shaker Village so near, then, to the sea?"

"Oh, Charlie," hiding her face on my shoulder, "that was cowardice in me. You know I meant to keep the cottage open and live there. It was the saddest place in all the world, but still I wanted to be there - alone. But I found I could not be alone; and the last people who came drove me nearly wild - those R - s, Fanny Meyrick's friends - and they talked about her and about you, so that I could bear it no longer. I wanted to hide myself from all the world. I knew I could be quiet at the Shaker village. I had often driven over there with Aunt Sloman: indeed, Sophia - that's the one you saw - is a great friend of Aunt Maria's."

"So the lady-abbess confessed, did she?" I asked with some curiosity.

"Yes: she said you were rudely inquisitive; but she excused you as unfamiliar with Shaker ways."

"And were you really at Watervliet?"

"Yes, but don't be in a hurry: we'll come to that presently. Sophia gave me a pretty little room opening out of hers, and they all treated me with great kindness, if they *did* call me Eliza."

"And did you," I asked with some impatience, remembering Hiram's description - "did you sew beads on velvet and plait straw for mats?"

Sarah C. Hallowell

"Nonsense! I did whatever I pleased. I was parlor-boarder, as they say in the schools. But I did learn something, sir, from that dear old sister Martha. You saw *her*?"

"The motherly body who invited me in?"

"Yes: isn't she a dear? I took lessons from her in all sorts of cookery: you shall see, Charlie, I've profited by being a Shakeress."

"Yes, my darling, but did you - you didn't go to church?"

"Only once," she said, with a shiver that made her all the dearer, "and they preached such dreary stuff that I told Sophia I would never go again."

"But did you really wear that dress I saw you in?"

"For that once only. You see, I was at Watervliet when you came. If you had only gone straight there, dear goose! instead of dodging in the road, you would have found me. I had grown a little tired of the monotony of the village, and was glad to join the party starting for Niskayuna, it was such a glorious drive across the mountain. I longed for you all the time."

"Pretty little Shakeress! But why did they put us on such a false track?"

"Oh, we had expected to reach home that night, but one of the horses was lame, and we did not start as soon as we had planned. We came back on Saturday afternoon - Saturday afternoon, and this is Monday morning!", leaning back dreamily, and looking across the blue distance to the far-off hills. "Then I got your card, and they told me about you, and I knew, for all the message, that you'd be back on Sunday morning. But how could I tell then that Fanny Meyrick would not be with you?"

"Bessie!" and my hand tightened on hers.

"Oh, Charlie, you don't know what it is to be jealous. Of course I did know that - no, I didn't, either, though I must have been *sure* underneath that day. For it was more in fun than anything else, after I knew you were in the meeting-house -"

"How did you know?"

"I saw you drive up - you and Hiram and Mrs. Hiram."

"You didn't think, then, that it was Mrs. Charles?"

"So I stole into Sophia's room, and put on one of her dresses. She is tall too, but it did not fit very well."

"I should think not," I answered, looking down admiringly at her.

"In fact," laughing, "I took quite a time pinning myself into it and getting the neckerchief folded prim. I waited till after the sermon, and then I knew by the singing that it was the last hymn, so I darted in. I don't know what they thought - that I was suddenly converted, I suppose, and they would probably have given thanks over me as a brand snatched from the burning. Did I do the dance well? I didn't want to put them out."

"My darling, it was a dreadful masquerade. Did you want to punish me to the end?"

"I was punished myself, Charlie, when you fell. Oh dear! don't let's talk about the dreadful thing any more. But I think you would have forgiven Elder Nebson if you had seen how tenderly he lifted you into the wagon. There, now: where are we going to live in New York, and what have we got to live on besides my little income?"

"Income! I had forgotten you had any."

"Ask Judge Hubbard if I haven't. You'll see."

"But, my dear," said I gravely, drawing forth the packet from my breast, "I, too, have my story to tell. I cannot call it a confession, either; rather it is the story of somebody else - Hallo! who's broken the seal?" For on shipboard I had beguiled the time by writing a sort of journal to accompany Fanny's letter, and had placed all together in a thick white envelope, addressing it, in legal parlance, "To whom it may concern."

"*I* did," said Bessie faintly, burying her face on my arm. "It fell out of your pocket when they carried you up stairs; and I read it, every word, twice over, before you came to yourself."

"You little witch! And I thought you were marrying me out of pure faith in me, and not of sight or knowledge."

"It was faith, the highest faith," said Bessie proudly, and looking into my eyes with her old saucy dash, "to know, to feel sure, that that sealed paper concerned nobody but me."

And so she has ever since maintained.

Choose from Thousands of 1stWorldLibrary Classics By

Ada Leverson
Adolphus William Ward
Aesop
Agatha Christie
Alexander Aaronsohn
Alexander Kielland
Alexandre Dumas
Alfred Gatty
Alfred Ollivant
Alice Duer Miller
Alice Turner Curtis
Alice Dunbar
Ambrose Bierce
Amelia E. Barr
Andrew Lang
Andrew McFarland Davis
Andy Adams
Anna Sewell
Annie Besant
Annie Hamilton Donnell
Annie Payson Call
Annonaymous
Anton Chekhov
Arnold Bennett
Arthur Conan Doyle
Arthur M. Winfield
Arthur Ransome
Atticus
B.H. Baden-Powell
B. M. Bower
Baroness Emmuska Orczy
Baroness Orczy
Basil King
Bayard Taylor
Ben Macomber
Bertha Muzzy Bower
Bjornstjerne Bjornson
Booth Tarkington
Boyd Cable
Bram Stoker
C. Collodi
C. E. Orr
C. M. Ingleby
Carolyn Wells
Catherine Parr Traill
Charles A. Eastman
Charles Dickens
Charles Dudley Warner
Charles Farrar Browne

Charles Ives
Charles Kingsley
Charles Klein
Charles Lathrop Pack
Charles Whibley
Charles Willing Beale
Charlotte M. Braeme
Charlotte M. Yonge
Charlotte Perkins Stetson
Clair W. Hayes
Clarence Day Jr.
Clarence E. Mulford
Clemence Housman
Confucius
Cornelis DeWitt Wilcox
Cyril Burleigh
D. H. Lawrence
Daniel Defoe
David Garnett
Don Carlos Janes
Donald Keyhoe
Dorothy Kilner
Dougan Clark
Douglas Fairbanks
E. Nesbit
E.P.Roe
E. Phillips Oppenheim
Edgar Rice Burroughs
Edith Van Dyne
Edith Wharton
Edward J. O'Biren
Edward S. Ellis
Edwin L. Arnold
Eleanor Atkins
Eliot Gregory
Elizabeth Gaskell
Elizabeth McCracken
Elizabeth Von Arnim
Ellem Key
Emerson Hough
Emily Dickinson
Enid Bagnold
Enilor Macartney Lane
Erasmus W. Jones
Ernie Howard Pie
Ethel Turner
Ethel Watts Mumford
Eugenie Foa
Eugene Wood

Evelyn Everett-green
Everard Cotes
F. H. Cheley
F. J. Cross
Federick Austin Ogg
Ferdinand Ossendowski
Francis Bacon
Francis Darwin
Frances Hodgson Burnett
Frances Parkinson Keyes
Frank Gee Patchin
Frank Harris
Frank Jewett Mather
Frank L. Packard
Frank V. Webster
Frederic Stewart Isham
Frederick Trevor Hill
Frederick Winslow Taylor
Friedrich Kerst
Friedrich Nietzsche
Fyodor Dostoyevsky
G.A. Henty
G.K. Chesterton
Gabrielle E. Jackson
Garrett P. Serviss
Gaston Leroux
George Ade
Geroge Bernard Shaw
George Durston
George Ebers
George Eliot
George MacDonald
George Meredith
George Orwell
George Tucker
George W. Cable
George Wharton James
Gertrude Atherton
Grace E. King
Grace Gallatin
Grant Allen
Guillermo A. Sherwell
Gulielma Zollinger
Gustav Flaubert
H. A. Cody
H. B. Irving
H.C. Bailey
H. G. Wells
H. H. Munro

H. Irving Hancock
H. Rider Haggard
H. W. C. Davis
Hamilton Wright Mabie
Hans Christian Andersen
Harold Avery
Harold McGrath
Harriet Beecher Stowe
Harry Houidini
Helent Hunt Jackson
Helen Nicolay
Hendrik Conscience
Hendy David Thoreau
Henri Barbusse
Henrik Ibsen
Henry Adams
Henry Ford
Henry Frost
Henry James
Henry Jones Ford
Henry Seton Merriman
Henry W Longfellow
Herbert A. Giles
Herbert N. Casson
Herman Hesse
Homer
Honore De Balzac
Horace Walpole
Horatio Alger Jr.
Howard Pyle
Howard R. Garis
Hugh Lofting
Hugh Walpole
Humphry Ward
Ian Maclaren
Inez Haynes Gillmore
Irving Bacheller
Israel Abrahams
Ivan Turgenev
J.G.Austin
J. Henri Fabre
J. M. Barrie
J. Macdonald Oxley
J. S. Fletcher
J. S. Knowles
J. Storer Clouston
Jack London
Jacob Abbott
James Allen
James Andrews
James Baldwin

James DeMille
James Joyce
James Lane Allen
James Lane Allen
James Oliver Curwood
James Oppenheim
James Otis
James R. Driscoll
Jane Austen
Jens Peter Jacobsen
Jerome K. Jerome
John Burroughs
John Cournos
John F. Kennedy
John Gay
John Glasworthy
John Habberton
John Joy Bell
John Kendrick Bangs
John Milton
John Philip Sousa
Jonas Lauritz Idemil Lie
Jonathan Swift
Joseph A. Altsheler
Joseph Carey
Joseph Conrad
Joseph E. Badger Jr
Joseph Hergesheimer
Joseph Jacobs
Julian Hawthrone
Julies Vernes
Justin Huntly McCarthy
Kakuzo Okakura
Kenneth Grahame
Kenneth McGaffey
Kate Langley Bosher
Kate Langley Bosher
Katherine Cecil Thurston
Katherine Stokes
L. A. Abbot
L. T. Meade
L. Frank Baum
Latta Griswold
Laura Lee Hope
Laurence Housman
Leo Tolstoy
Leonid Andreyev
Lewis Carroll
Lilian Bell
Lloyd Osbourne
Louis Tracy

Louisa May Alcott
Lucy Fitch Perkins
Lucy Maud Montgomery
Lydia Miller Middleton
Lyndon Orr
M. Corvus
M. H. Adams
Margaret E. Sangster
Margaret Vandercook
Margret Penrose
Maria Edgeworth
Maria Thompson Daviess
Mariano Azuela
Marion Polk Angellotti
Mark Overton
Mark Twain
Mary Austin
Mary Catherine Crowley
Mary Cole
Mary Hastings Bradley
Mary Roberts Rinehart
Mary Rowlandson
M. Wollstonecraft Shelley
Maud Lindsay
Max Beerbohm
Myra Kelly
Nathaniel Hawthrone
Nicolo Machiavelli
O. F. Walton
Oscar Wilde
Owen Johnson
P.G. Wodehouse
Paul and Mabel Thorne
Paul G. Tomlinson
Paul Severing
Percy Brebner
Peter B. Kyne
Plato
R. Derby Holmes
R. L. Stevenson
R. S. Ball
Rabindranath Tagore
Rahul Alvares
Ralph Henry Barbour
Ralph Waldo Emmerson
Rene Descartes
Rex Beach
Rex E. Beach
Richard Harding Davis
Richard Jefferies
Richard Le Gallienne

Robert Barr
Robert Frost
Robert Gordon Anderson
Robert L. Drake
Robert Lansing
Robert Lynd
Robert Michael Ballantyne
Robert W. Chambers
Rosa Nouchette Carey
Rudyard Kipling
Samuel B. Allison
Samuel Hopkins Adams
Sarah Bernhardt
Selma Lagerlof
Sherwood Anderson
Sigmund Freud
Standish O'Grady
Stanley Weyman
Stella Benson
Stephen Crane
Stewart Edward White
Stijn Streuvels
Swami Abhedananda

Swami Parmananda
T. S. Ackland
T. S. Arthur
The Princess Der Ling
Thomas A. Janvier
Thomas A Kempis
Thomas Anderton
Thomas Bailey Aldrich
Thomas Bulfinch
Thomas De Quincey
Thomas H. Huxley
Thomas Hardy
Thomas More
Thornton W. Burgess
U. S. Grant
Valentine Williams
Various Authors
Victor Appleton
Virginia Woolf
Walter Camp
Walter Scott
Washington Irving
Wilbur Lawton

Wilkie Collins
Willa Cather
Willard F. Baker
William Dean Howells
William le Queux
W. Makepeace Thackeray
William W. Walter
Winston Churchill
Yei Theodora Ozaki
Yogi Ramacharaka
Young E. Allison
Zane Grey